MW00989898

HARALD VOETMANN

Awake

translated from the Danish
by Johanne Sorgenfri Ottosen

 A NEW DIRECTIONS PAPERBOOK

Originally published in Danish by Gyldendal in 2010

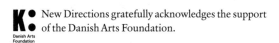 New Directions gratefully acknowledges the support of the Danish Arts Foundation.

Danish Arts
Foundation

The two letters in the appendix are drawn from *The Letters of Pliny the Younger*, translated by Betty Radice and published by Penguin Classics. Reprinted by permission of Penguin Books Limited

Manufactured in the United States of America
First published in 2021 as New Directions Paperbook 1511
Design by Erik Rieselbach

Library of Congress Cataloging-in-Publication Data
Names: Voetmann, Harald, 1978– author. |
Ottosen, Johanne Sorgenfri, 1986– translator.
Title: Awake / Harald Voetmann ; translated from the Danish
by Johanne Sorgenfri Ottosen.
Other titles: Vågen. English
Description: New York : New Directions Publishing Corporation, 2021.
Identifiers: LCCN 2021022110 | ISBN 9780811230810 (paperback) |
ISBN 9780811230827 (ebook)
Subjects: LCSH: Pliny, the Elder—Fiction. | LCGFT: Biographical fiction. |
Novels.
Classification: LCC PT8177.32.O38 V3413 2021 | DDC 839.813/8—dc23
LC record available at https://lccn.loc.gov/2021022110

10 9 8 7 6 5 4 3 2 1

New Directions Books are published for James Laughlin
by New Directions Publishing Corporation
80 Eighth Avenue, New York 10011

1

It is the same to me where I begin for I shall go back there again.
—Parmenides of Elea

It is the same to me where I begin for I shall go back there again. I shall go back to where I began. To the finding, in this case. I shall return to the finding that it is of no relevance where we begin. Though it must be said that this particular beginning—the moment when we first noted that we can begin anywhere, in turn granting each beginning its own irrelevance, yes, its very own —is more striking than others after all because it springs from a truth despite landing in falsehood. When I return to the point where we established the irrelevance of beginnings, the point is no longer a beginning. It is no longer subjected to the irrelevance of beginnings, but to the more general irrelevance of the whole, which naturally includes the point of beginning itself, which thereby loses all, or part, of its distinction. Wherefrom holds no more meaning than whereto, wherefore, where. "To," indeed, "to" is the purest expression of irrelevance— to all this I shall return. Look around. There's room here, and opportunity, you need only crane your neck to see what's on offer. What it all comes down to is glimpsing something worth craning your neck for. Preferably far enough that if the head was severed from the outstretched and so proffered neck there would be ample time to marvel at it spinning toward the desired object. The animals here refuse to let my

3

body sleep off the wine and my work suffers for it. At dawn, the cocks on the mountainside crow, then the cocks by the coast respond, and soon after the birds initiate their trilling in the sky before, worst of all, the dogs launch into rabid barking. By noon I am too drained to continue my work. I will have a bite of bread, perhaps an egg, then at least no cock will hatch from it, and drink the day's first cup of wine. Otherwise any attempt at sleep is futile. At about this point human noises intrude. All human acts can be sorted into three groups: work, play, and sex. Apart from that there is only rest, which includes any revitalization of the body such as bathing and supping, but rest, as we know, is not an act. Upon further scrutiny we may narrow down the three categories. Play is training and education, and a child's play is in large measure serious. Play is labor too. Sex can be either play or labor depending on the participant's role and reasons for taking part, but as we have eliminated the category of play, there is only one option left. Sexual activity can only be defined as a kind of labor, and all participants would do well to strive for the superior work ethic of the slaves who know they must endure it. You won't hear them cursing and fuming and acting out while others are trying to nap—trouble springs from the perceived masters of the situation who trust that their ejaculation, under the right circumstances, is for pleasure, and never realize that their urge is but earthly slavery imposed on them. I shall come back to this. Presently we are left with one category that encompasses all human activity not counting the body's revitalization. That category is labor. The body rests in preparation for labor, and rest can hereby be considered an activity in and of itself, which is to say part of the activity since only one activity, labor, exists. As labor goes, rest is no more passive than whatever else is imposed on us to endure, i.e. toiling at the grain mill, or being mounted by one's owner. Let the toiling take solace in the fact that the world only has one ruler, and tyrants and cutthroats are governed by it too. And by this force, the cock crows, the prick throbs, the dog barks. I don't know this despot's name, but I curse it day in and day out. I rarely get my afternoon nap, even after drinking wine. Instead, I toss and turn for hours, and once roused only wine can lift the headache of prior consumption. By evening I don't always succeed in making meaningful conversation. When I arrived in this town my reputation of wisdom gained abroad preceded me. The reputation still holds though it is wearing thin. Now, right now, as I was dictating this, a bird shat on my hand. My cue, perhaps. Perhaps some authority is attempting to impart how meaningless it is to curse it. But why would it bother? Better to establish irrelevance and to incessantly classify it until your tissue has hornified from inside out, than to curse and fume. From this point on you may be considered wise, but don't get overexcited. The bird's dropping is yellow and thin with a dense white lump at the center, which, upon closer inspection, will probably turn out to contain a sort of kernel. A seed. By way of a bird's behind a berry has ejaculated on me. But the seed has fallen on barren ground. My hand will not sprout. My hand shall not make anything sprout.

The little houses and tombs by the coast are indistinguishable from up here on the mountainside. Little red-tiled blocks all. The necropolis lies closer to the sea whereas the living have settled up the incline. For that reason alone, I can tell them apart. Each morning the fishermen pass through the city of the dead with their nets. And the children scramble by naked on their way to bathe in the sea. At night a few come out to make bonfires for their dead and the beggars stand by to partake of the sacrifice along with the basest of whores, those who sleep in the houses of the dead by day and come out at dusk to mate with the living for a slab of the deads' food. I can't sleep off the wine for all the shrieking animals between the small, dense olive trees on the slope. Tonight, it was the dogs. The black bitch who roams the hills with her extensive litter, the offspring of at least two fathers by the looks of them, howled louder than I could stand. I sent Hermeros out with an oar to chase her away. His arm was bleeding when he returned, she'd sunk her teeth deep in him. He said the bitch had been howling over a pup crushed by the children with their clubs, and now she wouldn't be chased off. Pound as he might with his oar, in her grief she took the beating but refused to let him shove her down the slope and away from the remains of her pup. Hermeros looks pleased as he writes this, as if putting his name in writing has now absolved him of all mortality. When I arrived here by ship, the first sight I encountered was the necropolis, the town's face. Stelas inscribed with the names of those who couldn't come to greet me. By each stela a signpost warns not to defecate near this tomb, that ghosts and furies and fiends of the underworld will surely beleaguer the one who parts his cheeks and ejects the modest portion of death stored in his guts among the dead. The innards of the dead are different, crawling with life for as long as it survives. The only sacrifice I will ask for myself is the death amassed throughout the day. Bequeath it to my grave, with my compliments, if you wish. The hiss of the cicadas is in the air. I've come to drink and impress the crowd, not to think, that's impossible, nothing will come of it. Thought separates the living from the dead. All life bred in the heat of the earth under the dense olive trees. Death is cold, it's the result of thought, one might regard it as the sigil of experience. One should never end an address to other people, written or spoken, with allusions to death. It's implicit, it makes itself known once the mouth has shut. It ought to be enough to point out the trivial and let its opposite speak. The more chatter about trifles, the more violent the contrast. Through speech, death bemoans its lack of trivialities. Infernal cicadas, i.e.

2

Voices

Quotes from Pliny the Elder's *Naturalis Historia*
Pliny the Elder
Pliny the Younger
Diocles, a slave

Quote, Naturalis Historia by Pliny the Elder

I simply wish to remind the reader that I am in a rush to describe the world in detail.

Scene I

Plinius has a nosebleed. He's lying on his back in bed, staring into the dark. Diocles stuffs his nostrils with wool soaked in rose oil. Plinius breathes heavily, his throat wheezes at each inhalation. The light is too dim to reach the ceiling. Diocles wipes his oiled fingers against his tunic and returns to the desk with the lamp, the tablets and the stylus. Punic beeswax is superior, snorts Plinius, and the stylus scratches in the tablet's wax, which is inferior; dingy and grimy, worn by countless smudgings. Diocles has taught his scribing hand to listen, only fragments of the world catch his mind. In the gloom it's impossible to gauge how high the ceiling is. To Plinius it feels as though it heaves above him in accordance with his troubled breathing. He is lying flat on his back with a pillow supporting his neck. His hands are resting to either side. On the matter of beeswax, one must pursue the deepest yellow of color, the kind that smells most intensely honeyed, he says. The final syllable of each sentence is extracted and rounded perfectly as it slowly transforms into a moan. Painfully and peepingly, the world is wrung from Plinius' fat neck in the dark. Now he lifts his left hand and puts his palm against the wall, which is cool and smooth, perfectly motionless.

Quote, Naturalis Historia

The sun's rising and setting leave no doubt that our orb-shaped world rotates in an eternal circuit, and at inconceivable speed, completing each trip within twenty-four hours. I can hardly guess whether the whir of so great a mass transcends the faculty of human hearing, nor do I know, by Hercules, if the stars that are swept along and revolve in their own orbits produce a timbre, and if so, whether it is a harmony of indescribable beauty. To us who live inside it, the world appears to glide in silence day and night.

Pliny the Elder

On the great construction site where my father built the new theater, treadmill cranes abounded. An especially squalid kind of slave worked in the treadmills. They spoke neither Greek nor Latin, not a word, and they would never know what a theater is. It wasn't so much the sight of the naked, sweaty bodies thrusting themselves forward and up incessantly, caught in the spinning wheel that transmitted their motions to the large stones waiting to be hoisted up. It was the sounds; the smacks of their flesh slapping the boards moment after moment, their moans and wails and incomprehensible muttered curses. That is precisely how I imagine the noise of the universe. The planets and stars lashed to their orbits while the ropes and coils and pulleys creak. Pythagoras must be mad to speak of cosmic harmonies.

The noise of the universe to me has always been the sound of something heavy and solid, hauled by Germanic and Numidian treadmill slaves. A constant sound of strain only surpassed occasionally by the lash of the whip. The pure, exalted ether that grudgingly turns to befouled air, and then to water, before with utter abandon it becomes earth, clay, flesh, and stone till it has squashed itself so compact, kneaded its own material so massively, that the spirit seeps from it and, as ether, ascends again to the sky with a sigh of relief. From the colonnade in the square where I received my lessons, I could observe the slaves work and hear it all. It was the habitual background noise as I sat in the shade and studied Greek verse on the creation of the gods and the siege of Troy. I only toiled with clusters of word and thought held together by my breath, by pure spirit. Homer's and Hesiod's knobbly and duly suckled immortalities on my tongue, in the shade, in the colonnade, in the square in Novum Comum. Just as with the slaves' labor in the treadmills, the purpose of my labor was to give life and motion to the dead; dead spirit in my case, dead matter in theirs. On a late summer afternoon a slave died in a treadmill, he breathed the spirit from its vessel, was refined and ascended, commingled with the luminous ether above us. He was dead midway through a motion intended for the stone, and some time passed before it was noticed. The other two slaves in the treadmill continued their crawling forth and up and nowhere. The deceased, who had been worming away in the same manner, was turned on his back, boards pounded against the base of his head where the skull and spine adjoin. He did not react. His body was cast from the treadmill and another slave was undressed and inserted. The corpse remained there the entire afternoon, in the sun, right in the middle of the construction site. On its back, its torso twisted. One eye shut, the other open, dark blue, Germanic, turned to the sky. The strain and the complete stillness, the strain's result. The wheel kept spinning next to the corpse, transmitting the motions of the living onto dead matter. I dare say that the theater, upon its completion, never staged a production as significant.

Quote, Naturalis Historia

The tallest man of our time was Gabbara, brought here from Arabia during the reign of the Divine Claudius—he stood nine foot and nine inches tall. In the reign of Augustus there were two who exceeded him by half a foot, Pusio and Secundilla, their remarkable bodies preserved as objects of curiosity in a tomb in the Gardens of Sallust.

Pliny the Elder

It was before I had seen anyone die or anyone kill. It was before I had slipped from the hands of my mother and my wet nurse to my father and his peers in the square. It was summer, choking heat, and I clung to my mother's skirts. We strolled the long avenues in the Gardens of Sallust, newly opened to the public, and greeted the other mothers and children politely. A couple of shy toddlers meeting each other for the first time hide behind their mothers, clutching their dresses and peeking behind their thighs. The looks two such children will give each other. Were it in their power to kill, they would. Pine, poplar, platanus. Cool marble benches in the shade where the old women with their impatient grandchildren paused to catch breath. The narrow, steep paths between the levels of landscaping, the umber dust whirling and settling on sandals and feet and in the pleat of a toga's hem. The street vendors and trinket sellers hawking: Salvé, domina! My mother bought me a little donkey made of red clay. The donkey dangled on a leather strap, it was meant as a necklace. My mother tightened the strap so that I might wear it around my wrist instead where it wouldn't eclipse the golden orb on my chest that marked my class. The trinket seller's skin was dark and blotchy from exposure to sun and dust. His accent was Greek, his copper hoops were green with verdigris. He bent down toward me with some difficulty, rested his hands on his knees and said: "The donkey is a diligent animal, let it serve to remind you of the virtue of diligence, my friend. Toil, little donkey, it shall serve you well." From a breast pocket in his tunic, he produced a fig and gave it to me with a stiff smile. The fig was bruised. "Say thank you to the gentleman," said my mother. But he was no gentleman. And the donkey he had sold us was shaped by children's hands, not by this Greek's clumsy, dirty fingers. You could see the unsmoothed dents left by small fingertips in the clay. Toil, little donkey. The Greek sold clay figures in the Gardens of Sallust all day, every day, and somewhere his children were manufacturing them in heaps. The small animal had been crafted without love or curiosity, and although I'd pleaded with my mother to have it only minutes prior, I suddenly wanted to smash it. It looked nothing like a donkey. The neck was too short and fat. The legs were crooked and uneven, it wouldn't even be able to stand upright. The eyes were off. It had no nostrils. "How can this inspire diligence? It is so poorly done," I said. The columns, nailed full of bulletins; acta diurna; gossip, weddings and divorces, the size of someone's dowry, what does he see in her, finally a decent drinking fountain in Subura, have you heard whose husband has been elected tribune; prophecies and interpretations of the night sky, good news for anyone with husbands and sons in Germania, news bulletins nailed to thick trunks along the avenues, esteemed ladies, wigmaker Marius Scorius on Esquiline will gladly compensate you for your locks of hair, make a little extra for the household, real Egyptian cosmetics, stimulate your husband with Nubian drum dancing, performed at the court to great applause, hair removal, cheap and painless, undesirable bodily circumstances treated at no health risk, blood curses purged, bring a cock or a black puppy for sacrificing, would you happen to know the best fish sauce in town, hire a choir to lament your dead, gemstones and paintings, the most beautiful ivory miniatures in walnut shells, have your ancestral history written in Greek or Latin. So was the world of women that I was steered through. I'd barely learned how to read but with each sign I exercised my new skill. What more? Everywhere, muddy puddles and hosts of insects. Flies, midges, mosquitoes, wasps, but also dragonflies. I remember one dragonfly mounting another's back. They buzzed around in this formation for a distance, lazily keeping to a somewhat wobbly course. I imagined they were mating, I suppose they were. But suddenly the top dragonfly lifted while the other dropped limply to the ground in a straight line. I collected it in my hand, it filled my palm. I could see a puncture on its neck. I shuddered more profoundly at the sight than I would at any of the later battles of beasts or gladiators my father and his peers let me watch from the equestrian seats. Never, not among the Greeks nor our own writers, have I stumbled upon a piece that told of the dragonfly's mating ritual. Was the murder an expression of the male's arousal? Or was it that, during copulation, he deemed the female unworthy of his brood? Or was she punished for resisting? I find it hard to believe that the Greeks should not have observed the phenomenon, and it isn't unreasonable to suggest the following explanation, that the Greek dragonflies would simply never kill during mating, that this is only seen in Italy. A group of pavilions concluded the Gardens' broadest avenue, they were built by Julia, granddaughter of Augustus, before she fell from grace. Here lay dead monstrosities of the court, on display to throngs of women and children, embalmed and stuffed with scented textiles, sandalwood, cloves and nard. The pavilions formed a circle with the largest at the center, inside the bodies of Pusio and Secundilla hung from hooks in the ceiling. It defies all probability that these two giants should have emerged from different corners of the Earth and not be related by blood, but it is said that Secundilla was from Thrace while Pusio came from Ethiopia. They were the same height, and their hanging bodies spanned the length of the pavilion, floor to ceiling. Their forms were thin, their skin dark purple and crinkled like the bruised fig the salesman had given me, and which I would not eat but was afraid to discard fearing a slap from my mother for my ingratitude. Though Pusio's skin must have been black when he was alive, he was now no darker than Secundilla. Because of the hooks in their necks they both hung with their faces down and their arms flaccid along their sides as though they were ashamed. The look of shame was enhanced by the stare in their painted glass eyes, at once dead and panic-stricken. Both had arms too short for their long bodies, making it look as though they were grasping for their genitals, but could not quite reach. Pusio gave the impression of wishing to cover his purple and unevenly stuffed penis while Secundilla looked to be grasping indecently for her crotch, an obscene gesture. Secundilla's thighs and buttocks were very full and round but otherwise the bodies were like sticks, and I believe that any roundness may have been artificial, manufactured postmortem so the observer could discern, closely and from a distance, which one of these desiccated creatures had been a woman. Their wretched postures instilled in me the thought that their contortion might be a conscious act—that these creatures were willfully contorted: one wishing to conceal his shame, the other trying to expose it fully. My mother put her hand on my hair and bent over me. She laughed, she probably found the sight amusing. "Can you believe a person can grow that big, Gaius," she whispered in my ear, and all around the pavilion women stood and whispered like that into the ears of their children or grandchildren. But I didn't find it funny. My mother's laugh mirrored another laughter. Through her, nature mocked these freaks created for the purpose of ridicule and ghastly deformity. That day I had my fill of the women's world.

Quote, Naturalis Historia

Is poison not born out of man's brutality? The gloomy tongue of man flickers like the serpent, and the gangrene of impure minds consumes everything it touches, and like the winged harbingers of ill, they disrupt their own element—the silence of darkness and night—with wailing, the only sound they can utter; we are greeted by these ominous beasts who forbid us to act or aid the living. They know of no other way to pay back the world for their abject souls than to despise everything.

Pliny the Elder

It's not difficult to imagine the world's end. The difficult part is to imagine that *right here* will be nothing. The inferno that our age rushes to meet is palpable in the soul's hatred of itself and of the world. That the world will one day despise itself to death is not worth our tears and no amount of tears could put out the flames. There are reports of self-ignition caused by shame. When Appius Claudius decimated his army after its ignominious defeat against the Volscians, it is said that several of the soldiers who had not been picked for execution burst into flames in recognition of their share of the blame. There are numerous such stories of spontaneous combustion in connection to drinking and gambling, and in the schools it also appears to be common. However, we have yet to hear of women and animals who hate themselves aflame. Animals, that should come as no surprise. The scorned bull or stallion will unleash his rage freely on the world, and is, for that matter, hardly conscious enough to hate himself. To loathe oneself, one must be able to judge oneself according to the standards of peers and ancestors. It's different with women. I would not go so far as to suggest that women are more shameless than men as several examples of the female pudicitia exist, but perhaps their shame is more general, shame felt on behalf of an entire species rather than the individual alone. Even as they indulge their shame and allow themselves to go mad with desire for blood-splattered gladiators and dusty donkey herders, it can hardly be considered personal.

That the drive to copulate in man should be so entwined with self-loathing is unique; many seek oblivion in mating. And the fire spreads. The world, the damned pyre, is expanding. And not just in size, knowledge of the world expands too, and with it the extent to which it despises itself. In its attempt to burn out, the fire always catches another fragment of the void and the flames spread. Soon it will have spread so far that no one will see an end to it and no library will withstand the destruction.

Pliny the Younger

My uncle was neither a poet nor a philosopher. But he was a diligent and conscientious commander. He worked his way up from perhaps not entirely modest means, but still. His literary work is no less capricious than nature, and as with nature, it is sometimes indecisive and at war with itself.

Pliny the Elder

Fire can easily envision its own end, burning out is the cause it has worked for all along. It is the thought of those left behind that causes pain. That the place where everything was incinerated will still exist. That someone will poke around in the ashes and discover that we have not done enough. Traces remain after the world's great bonfire. All we can hope is that someone will gather what remains or brush it away, and not condemn us for what we left behind; the many small traces of inadequate self-hatred and unacknowledged vileness. No, by Hercules, it's a lie. The only thing we can hope for is that no one will rise from the ashes.

Quote, Naturalis Historia

Below the eyebrows are the eyes, the body's most precious component, which by their use of light disclose the difference between life and death.

Pliny the Elder

I am in the front row of a seedy theater constructed with oak planks. There is a barrier in front of me which surrounds the stage. The next thirteen rows, rising behind me, do not look solid. Only bloodlust can compel an audience to settle into something so unstable. They tower languidly though their weight makes the rows sway. The only emotion that seizes the crowd is anticipation. The spectator to my right presents himself as Mucianus. He tells me excitedly we're about to see a play in celebration of the double Diana. I tell him that I have seen the performance before, long ago. It wasn't any good. Mucianus is long-haired and unshaven—wisps of beard float around his face like furry mold on a bowl of soft, decaying cheese. He is wearing a coarse and soiled toga. Presently he turns his head away from me and looks upon the stage, which is covered with sand for the occasion. His left ear appears to be entirely sealed with yellow-brown wax. You wouldn't think he could hear anything through it. The wax glistens and it occurs to me that the theater is open, that the audience sits without protection from the baking noon sun—and the sun is high in the sky, the heat unbearable. Now I look closer, a word appears scratched into the glistening earwax, approximately in the center of Mucianus' large and moon-pale lump of an ear. The word must have been engraved carefully with a stylus as fine as a fly's leg. I lean in but I'm still unable to read the word—or perhaps there are several words. The letters shrink as I near them. The performance has begun. Mucianus can't sit still out of sheer excitement at what he's seeing. He twitches and hops in his seat and turns his head to and fro in swift jerks to catch all before him. I sigh in vexation, and abandon my attempt to read what's written inside his ear. Judging from his rough appearance, the message in his ear—if it is such a thing—is not likely to be terribly important. The five hundred or so people behind and above me scream, *habet, habet*. The first spatter of blood has hit the sand. A fat, ruddy savage stomps around in the sand in the costume of the goddess Diana with an amber wig and a woman's breast stitched onto the left side of his saffron tunic. He slices open the belly of a pregnant sow with a spear. She's howling and trying to flee. The contents flop out and trail after her in the sand, and yes, I can make out the young; a tiny bloody squirming clump that will be alive a few more moments. Diana has appeared to the sow in both her guises: the huntress and the deliverer. A wave of cheering erupts behind me. Mucianus applauds, mouth agape and eyes wide; what is it, scrawled inside his ear? The scene is repeated: a pregnant goat, a pregnant doe, a pregnant heifer, a pregnant mare, a pregnant wolf, it has taken hours now. Diana-Man hits the mark every time, cuts a long, deep gash across the belly which splits open under the weight from within, and out plop offspring and uterus, trailing in the sand for a stretch behind the wailing animal. The audience reacts with the same elation each time. The blood trails are indistinguishable by now, it is all a big stew through which Diana-Man wades, squelching and grunting. It is hard work and demands precision, and yet it's unbelievably dull to watch. The climax finally arrives: a pregnant woman is shoved onstage. Her breasts and crotch are covered but her belly is naked. She screams and tries to run. A jet of vomit is expelled from her mouth. A moment later, the spear pierces her belly, and as she scrambles away, hands covering her eyes, her belly opens, hesitantly, like a fat-lipped mouth about to utter an inconvenient truth. A hush descends on the auditorium. Everybody wishes to hear if the child just delivered by Diana screams, but how could anyone hear the screams of the baby over its mother's? I seize the opportunity. I grab a solid hold around Mucianus' chin with my left hand and clutch his long, wiry curls in my right. He freezes. Spare me, he says. I yank his head close to mine so that his left ear is right in front of my eyes. I read the message.

Quote, Naturalis Historia

Among the Roman augurs there is considerable debate regarding the birds known as sangualis and immusulus. Some hold that the immusulus is the vulture's young and the sangualis is the bonecrusher vulture's young. Masurius claims that while sangualis and the bonecrusher vulture are the same bird, that the immusulus is the eagle's young, before its tail turns white. Some have claimed that these birds have not been sighted in Rome since the augur Mucius' time—I myself find it more probable that due to a general sloppiness they have simply not been recognized.

Pliny the Elder

The urge to name and classify the world's miseries. Why else should we have been placed in their midst with this talent, this gift? Keep your eyes open and give each shade of pain and ghastliness its proper name. So that nature may acknowledge them. So that we may know her through them. Man has, uniquely among living creations, been granted the ability to learn the rules of nature's game, or at least some of them, or at least the ability to name the pieces. Who wants to end in the belly of an unidentified vulture species? Reserve namelessness for sweet-singing berry munchers and limpid ornamentals. Powder and perfume have no value except to teach us to recognize deception.

Pliny the Younger

My uncle gave me two goldfinches in a cage for my birthday
once. A few days later I tired of them and set them free. The
following year he gave me a gamecock.

Quote, Naturalis Historia

It is thought to bring good luck to spit into urine immediately upon discharging it.

Scene 2

Plinius awakens in the dark. The small round window in his bedroom is closed and he has no idea what time it is. The house is quiet. He knows the house well enough to be able to fumble his way out. He knows where the tiles slope and where to lower his head to avoid knocking into a beam. He walks barefoot in his sweat-soaked tunic, through the long corridor past kitchen and latrine and winter dining room, reaching the atrium where he can see the sky through the large, circular opening in the roof, and the sky is rose-colored and the marble tiles in the atrium are so cold and wet with dew he must temper his step to avoid slipping on them. For a moment he considers pissing in the impluvium—the large basin under the opening that receives rainwater—like he used to do as a boy when he wasn't permitted to go outside at night and was curbed by stories of bloodsucking screech owls and witches. The true dangers of the nocturnal streets were kept from him. He breathes deeply and continues into the other part of the house, through another long, dark corridor. When he finally arrives at the door, he has great trouble unbarring it, and it's made no easier by his escalating need to piss—the thought that he actually owns a house with a latrine, or that he might simply run back and relieve himself in the impluvium makes the need unbearable. But he wants to get out. He *has* to get out. He can't discern the walls or ceilings in here and being unable to see the limits of your prison is unbearable. He considers running back, all the way to the rear of the villa to wake the slaves, or maybe he could simply shout for them. Then he could go on with his work afterward, it's impossible to get anything done on your own. He finally manages to loosen the bar and it lands with a bang by his feet. He thrusts the door open and scurries outside, into the fresh air and the fine rosy blue dawn. He urinates against a fig tree to the left of the front door with equal part relief and consternation at the immense pleasure of pissing on rather than into something. This doglike pleasure. There's no wind. He can hear the sea, very softly. And a flight of swallows above him heading for the coast. He looks at the house, all the darkness he possesses enclosed in heavy stones. No bloodsucking monster, no drunken cutthroat can make him go back in there. Not before the slaves are awake and the shutters have been lifted from all windows. The cool morning air tightens his throat. He puts a hand on the fig tree for support, bends over with his head between his knees and gasps, stares into the pool of yellow piss that starts to seep between his toes, glistening in the early light. His immense throat is obstructing the path to the lungs. They lie inside him, dark and secluded like his villa before him. They brood over the hot, foul air residing there. Blood drips from his nose to the piss between his feet. Thick, slimy blood that lies on the surface and spreads in squid-like shapes, slowly swirling and twining.

Quote, Naturalis Historia

I certainly do not believe that life is so valuable it must be prolonged at all costs. You who are of the opposite opinion will die nonetheless, even if your life has been prolonged by perverse acts and abominations. Therefore, let each take the following to be the soul's greatest remedy: Among all the gifts which nature has bestowed on man none surpass a timely death, and the best thing is that anyone can procure it for himself.

Pliny the Elder

The first gladiator games I remember attending were nothing more than harmless parades of weaponry, as is often the case in the small towns up north where no one can pay the lanista the cost of a death or a maiming. After my mother died attempting to rid herself of yet another one of the clumps whose origin I share, this all changed. My father, who suffered from the falling sickness—and mark you, this was not talked about—made a deal with each coming year's aedile to cover the cost of one death per spring. The games were held in the aedile's name and my father received no particular honors for the considerable sums he paid; only the rights over the body, which for one thing gave him access to drink the blood of the deceased, a treatment for the falling sickness that he had learned of during a stay in Rome, and for another gave him the right to sell the deceased's body parts as remedies for varied ills. Before the body was cold he'd have already put his lips to its wound and drunk from it, and by the end of day, many a mother would be rubbing her infected gums with a tooth from the dead warrior's mouth. Every year the price of these commodities increased, and the age, popularity, physical appearance, and general health of the deceased had no effect on the price, all that mattered was some hearsay that a lock of hair might arrest the advance of baldness, that a big toe carried in a leather strap around the neck could ease arthritis, a fingerbone avert the quartan fever, a testicle mashed and dissolved in vinegar promote fertility, a slice of tongue carried inside the mouth in a silver capsule protect against evil eyes and unrequited love, etc. It's my impression that no precisely defined system existed, but that both the nature of the superstition and my father's sales pitch depended on the ailment of the buyer. The business could be tailored to fit any shade of discomfort in life. The yearly expense of the death was soon amply covered. The gladiator games in Novum Comum, once a little arrangement in the square whose principal function was for the town notables to strut their finery for respective mobs of patrons and debtors and suck-ups, now drew audiences from other towns as well. Sick wretches all of them and none there to be entertained. A primitive amphitheater was erected on the town outskirts, behind the palaestra. It was a drained marsh and even in the hottest summer months the earth was blackish-green sludge. Fights were usually quick, if you slipped in the mud you were dead, and since someone always slipped before long, my father rarely had to compensate for the maiming of the winner. The body would be rushed onto a carriage. I would sit next to the coachman while my father lay coiled up with the body on the wagon bed, drinking from its wounds. A line of customers would have formed by our doorstep before we got there. Each year there was a new obsession. One person heard that the liver was the most effective cure for anything, and now the entire flock, the hundreds of poor sufferers, cried out for their right to buy a slice of liver. Another year, it would be the spleen or the fingernails. Naturally, nobody was let inside before all the blood was drained and everything had been cut up and grouped by price in tubs and on trays across the entire atrium. I have nothing more to say on this. When my father died, he had drunk the blood of sixteen gladiators, put his lips to their wounds and sucked. Maybe it kept him alive. I have nothing more to say on this.

Pliny the Younger

Gaius Plinius Caecilius Secundus greets his dear Baebius Macer.

I take from your response, which I received today and read with some measure of regret, that your interest in my uncle's works is not as general as you first led me to believe. Not satisfied with the index of his work that I provided for you, you demand to know whether among his notes there exists a description of his gardens at Tusculum. I understand that you have come into possession of these gardens. I will have you know that I do not intend to publish this letter, and should you harbor ambitions of letter-publishing yourself, I ask that you omit therein any reply to the letter at hand. That being said, I am now of a mind to start this letter again, slightly less formally.

Dear Baebius Macer. You set me a nearly inhuman task—to peruse my uncle's enormous collection of notes in order to find a description of a garden that likely passed into your ownership by the roll of a dice, but what do I care. I would not dream of obliging your request, and besides, I am not in possession of all his notes. If any are left at all. My dear Calpurnia has done away with a large portion of my library and replaced it with droning stories of Egyptian princesses and young lovers from Carthage or Milesian tales of a more sordid nature, enough even to make you blush. I have been forced to acquiesce after many quarrels. Calpurnia feared that her girlfriends might consider her uneducated, should they not see in our library the same titles they themselves read and use to furnish their ostentatious villas. And she feared, perhaps, that one of these women might happen to discover my uncle's notes or his Natural History and assume Calpurnia was interested in such ossified scholarship and fancy herself too elevated for the kind of literature they so eagerly discuss within their circle. Calpurnia would often snatch a scroll and begin reading it aloud to me, sneeringly, and with the sulking face of a little girl, to illustrate how it vexed her to live in a house full of books about stones and grain and trees and stars and insects. But as she stands there, in all her spite, I cannot be angry with her. She bends slightly to one side, slowly brushes her right foot against her left ankle. She is wearing one of my tunics and has tied it up with a belt in such a high place that her sex is right behind the purple trim. She pauses, bites her lower lip, and must concentrate in order to pronounce the long and peculiar words of the text while at the same time applying the right measure of scorn and disdain. On these occasions, all I wish to do is rip her clothes off and fuck her until this pretence is dispelled. For this, I should merrily burn down all the world's libraries.

So, the answer is no, my dear Baebius Macer, it is not possible for me to pore over my uncle's notes. Still, I can answer your inquiry with great certainty: No description of the gardens at Tusculum exists. And there is a particularly good reason behind it. The greater parts of the gardens which you now possess are established around unknown and undefined growths that my uncle had brought to him from all parts of the world. It was my uncle's close friendship with the Divine Vespasian that allowed him to build this collection of unknowns. The crew of any ship set for far-flung locales under imperial decree was charged with this extra task of bringing back the most exotic plants they could find.

As you know, my uncle wished to organize the world and in his Natural History he goes over its components minutely. It is an unparalleled feat to relay the world in writing, and one that I doubt could ever be repeated. However, my uncle must have suspected his project was doomed. He never examined the alien trees and flowers and shrubs in the garden at Tusculum, he never set foot among them, and he did not wish to be informed when something new was planted. I believe that the gardens at Tusculum were my uncle's attempt to contain the unknown, create a perimeter around it and become its master.

Only by the garden entrance, around the small cabin where we stayed on the rare occasions that we did visit, grew ordinary, familiar plants. Nice and dainty flowers in little squares like ranked soldiers, phalanxes of prettiness. It seems my uncle only appreciated the idea of loveliness when it was surrounded by something mysterious and menacing. In the evening, he would stand on the edge of this familiar and organized part of the garden and gaze off as the sun set. Rose, he would say. Always rose first. Then: Hyacinth. Oleander. Violet. Crocus. Peony. Buttercup. Lupine. Forget-me-not, etc. His spine was erect as he spoke the names of neat and well-known plants into the unknown beyond him. More than once he became furious during this process, sweat pouring from his forehead and eyes flashing, full of indignation, I believe that is the word. For the most part he was tense but collected. I have often wondered if such a string of flower names might not have been his final words. I cannot imagine what else he might say as he lay on the beach, staring into the void while Vesuvius showed him how it was merely the stem of a fire blossom whose crown reached into the sky, soon to let its thick, gray petals swaddle him.

There is no reason to drag this tale out further. But know

this, my dear Baebius Macer, that the gardens were intended to elude description and therefore are not mentioned in the briefest notation. Perhaps my uncle thought of the gardens as a sanctuary in the sense that this small part of the world and everything it contained needed not be relayed and explained as opposed to all else. And the more exotic plants were thrusted into those gardens, the larger my uncle's sanctuary, in a way. But as you can understand, this does not mean that its mere existence, let alone its expansion, did not make him anxious.

Many years have passed since I stood by my uncle's side and heard him shout the names of common flowers into the twilight and the unknown. I imagine that many of the exotic plants and trees have perished since they were not made to exist in our balmy climate but to fight for their lives in harsher terrains. Many species must have died, I believe, for the sole reason that there was no need to fight anymore. But others thrive, of course, and find plenty of strife among each other in their battle for the glorious Tusculan soil and the light of the sun. I doubt that the border between the known and the unknown is still distinct in the garden after all these years. Hyacinths and roses grow among Numidian desert plants, Hyperborean moss, and Indian giant trees.

My dear Baebius Macer. I know you do not fear the unknown, and you must know from our time in Syria that neither do I. But since you have come into possession of the gardens, I implore you to consider whether you're really capable of accepting that over time the border between the known and the unknown has been erased. And if you can't, what do you intend to do about it?

… beeswax as yellow as can be, honey-smelling, pure …

Pliny the Elder

There is something I must tell of our house in Novum Comum. And of my little sister, Plinia. Each year we received a large slab of Punic beeswax wrapped in papyrus and palm leaves. For it was always in the winter that Mother gave birth, at the start of each new year. Apart from Plinia and I, who came first, none of the children survived and all but two were stillborn. Our nurse Fulvia laboriously modelled a figure of each infant out of the Punic wax and these dolls were put up on the tablinum walls with the name and birth year on a bronze plaque beneath them. Where others put up masks of their ancestors, portraits of august forefathers who, like pearls on a string, proudly display the lineage's unbroken substance, we displayed in our house only the ceaseless potential of our lineage, yellow and honey-smelling. There were also two such dolls of Plinia and me on the wall. Both portrayed us sleeping peacefully. Two of the later dolls were fashioned with open, screaming mouths; this became Fulvia's way of showing that the child lived long enough to scream at the world. Whenever our parents were out of the house, Fulvia allowed us to unhook some of the dolls and take them down and play with them. I believe she let us do it out of some artistic pride; she wanted the dolls to be loved as dolls and not only revered as symbols. I can still see their little faces, and my own peaceful unfinished face hanging there. I can see Plinia in the atrium, in a dirty red tunic and with a long braid running down her neck. She is rocking the doll of a stillborn child in her arms, and she sings like our mother sang. I remember her impatience as our mother's belly grew. Every day she asked Fulvia when the next doll would come up, even though Fulvia would always shush her. Plinia and I only ever saw one of the children, the twelfth, the third last. Titus. He lay in his cot, his entire body laced in straps. Sometimes he screamed, mostly he stared into the ceiling or slept. During the spring his skin turned jaundiced as a sign that he too would soon be reduced to a yellow and honey-smelling sigil of potential. In the beginning of summer, only the doll remained, but this doll symbolized something to us. Plinia never played with that one.

Pliny the Younger

It is unlikely that my mother ever played with these dolls.

Quote, Naturalis Historia

I once saw Lollia Paulina, the wife of Emperor Gaius, covered with gleaming emeralds and pearls woven together, the jewels adorned her head, hair, ears, neck, and fingers, and were not worn at an illustrious or noteworthy ceremonial, but an ordinary betrothal dinner; altogether it was worth forty million sesterces, and she was prepared to prove her ownership of it at a moment's notice.

Pliny the Elder

And I once saw the third maniple of the cavalry's first cohort rape a Germanic boy in turn and leave him naked in the snow among the dead bodies of the burning village. I am not quite certain which of these sights I would rather have gone without.

Quote, Naturalis Historia

It is said that Zeuxis painted a boy carrying a handful of grapes, and when the birds targeted the grapes with a zest equal to before, he furiously approached his work and said "I have painted the grapes more convincingly than the boy, for had he been perfect, the birds would have feared him."

Pliny the Elder

How Lollia laughed that night. Through a curtain of jewels, her teeth shone. In the glow from the torches, the emeralds cast a greenish tinge on them.

Scene 3

Plinius has a nosebleed. He's lying on his back on the bed, staring into the dark. Diocles sprinkles his nostrils with pulverized nettle root, then stuffs them with wool soaked in rose oil. Plinius doesn't pause his dictation, he expects Diocles to catch up. In painful wheezes, the world is wrung from Plinius' fat neck in the dark. He speaks of mining in Hispania. A sentence or two may have been lost here. Diocles is thinking about how as a child he once glued the wings of a butterfly together with birdlime and then later regretted his deed. He won without a fight. The butterfly gave up instantly and fell to the ground on the spot where he'd thrown it, completely motionless. Now it's highly likely that a sentence about mining in Hispania has been lost because of Diocles' stray thought. Plinius' voice is reedy and obstructed. There's a womanish timbre to it, a womanish moan, it comes in a whimper from over there, from the bed in the darkness. Sometimes Diocles' prick stiffens at the sound of it, whenever he's tired, when he's been scribing for many hours and the words have ceased to register at all. On these occasions a sentence might have fallen away here and there. But sometimes, since he can't see fat old Plinius in the dark, the idea that it's a lustful woman lying on the bed, stroking her crotch obscenely, begins to dominate. Undeniably, errors might have been made on these occasions.

I have no doubt that much has been omitted. For I am merely a man and duties consume my days.

Diocles

I must have been having a nightmare. I don't remember exactly. What I remember is hearing a flight of twittering swallows heading for the coast. In an instant, I had the idea that each swallow carried in its beak a sliver of the dark dream in which I had been submerged, and that they were bringing it coastward for the rising sun to irradiate it, dissolve it into tiny, fluttery particles that the swallows might catch in their beaks again and feast on. I loved those swallows dearly. I felt grateful but also saddened. Though they had freed me of the dark dream, I still felt its residual darkness pounding in my head. I tried knocking on the door to the new kitchen maid's chamber, even if the sign on the door said she was menstruating. *Hiris! Hiris! Visne me fellare? Maestus sum,* I called. I took my aching prick in my hand and rubbed it against the door to her chamber, which is the closest it's been to her yet. It left a gleaming line like a snail's trail. That it is black bile doctors associate with sadness is difficult for me to understand. Nothing is more depressing than to be filled with semen to the point of bursting. Only at the body's expulsion of this seemingly light and life-giving matter, and in the happy cases its sowing, does the mind seem to brighten. Hiris hasn't sucked off anyone in the house yet, and she's had her menstruation sign up ever since she was acquired. Last night too all she answered was: *Nolo,* not aggressively, just drowsily, indolently. I remember resting my forehead against the door, sobbing. My prick was so full of darkness and I didn't know how I'd ever get anyone to swallow it, take it and do away with it so it wouldn't be *my* darkness anymore. The master can't help me in these matters. It would be impossible to ask him to ensure someone is available to me or Echion, the caretaker. The master doesn't understand us. It's only ears that he cares to penetrate with all his wheezy recitals. I sat down in the winter dining room where I knew a wine pitcher had been left out the day before. It was one of the silver pitchers ornamented with scenes. Maybe a gladiator fight, or something from Homer. It was too dark to make it out. The wine tasted terrible as always. Only those who haven't tried the sour wine served in our house will ever take my master's book on winemaking seriously. Damned book etched in filthy wax by these blistered hands. Then I was outside. I remember wondering if I was cold and being unable to determine it. I started following the path down the slope. I nearly slipped in the loose wet gravel several times, and I heard myself laugh about it. I carried the silver pitcher in my hand. How many women and boys would that buy in town? And not in the city of the dead, but in a good place; a place with room for snuggling and taking a nap after the emission, free from dreams. Where there is enough light so you can see your prick, see what you're thrusting into, and to see that it has to damn well take it. Somewhere on the horizon, my dark dream drifted in flakes over the sea and whirled into the surface foam.

Quote, Naturalis Historia

But what does the soul consist of? Which material? Where is its consciousness? How does it see, hear, and feel? How does it employ the senses, and what does it have to offer without them? And where do they live, these many centuries of souls and shadows, and how many are they? It is all but the childish lies of idiot mortals who greedily desire to never die.

Pliny the Elder

It is beyond doubt that man breaks down the food he ingests by way of heat, which is to say by way of the fire inside his being. But which faculty extracts the gainful matter and transmutes it into the flesh and fat of the human body while the useless matter is discharged? This cannot be by thermic powers alone. A portion of porridge sewn into a pig's belly, then heated, is not noticeably affected. Only a power that exists in life, though not in any of life's singular components, seems capable of splitting food into its useful, transmutable parts and its unavailing redundancies. Here, the word soul comes to mind, and precisely the ability to reign over matter and sort it into particulars characterizes the soul. But how does one imagine a soul that lives detached from the body, no longer able to perform its office through the body, from which we can only assume it derives its own nourishment?

Pliny the Younger

I remember clearly the experiment with the porridge in the pig's belly. My uncle asked me if I did not agree that one portion of the porridge would turn into shit, the other into pork. I said yes, solely to humor him, although my inherent good sense suspected otherwise. The porridge-stuffed belly was laid out in the sun for a few hours on a hot day. When we cut up the belly again the porridge was unchanged. Not until now did I realize what the experiment was truly about.

Quote, Naturalis Historia

And to think that among thousands of human beings there exist no two indistinguishable examples, and yet only ten features or so constitute our countenance.

Pliny the Elder

My face—ten or so features—appears to stare at me from *the depth* of the Corinthian bronze mirror. As though immersed in a basin filled with blood and water. It is staring at itself. I am staring at myself as though from the depth of a basin of blood and water, and I am staring at myself in the depth, and on. It is so simple and inexplicable. My face watches me watch it, watches it watch me. A description of my face would never evoke more than a summary of its parts and the same is true of any memory of it. Only when the face lies here before me does it amount to a fully-realized assertion, a sign that can be interpreted but not determined. A poem trussed in its own limping meter, from the glossy scalp to the chin's bumbling echoes down the neck. To think of it this way, from the top down, my face is a crash, a collapse. The tip of my head is pointed and from this tip the flesh cascades, gathering in pouches over the skull, whose orifices it seals over time, finally plunging over the chin with an abruptness that reverberates down the neck where the crash is repeated in ripples until the body, my trunk, begins.

Like ten eggs broken on the point of a spear, so oozes the flesh. One could also view it from the bottom up. From this perspective, the head strives upward into a peak from its wide root. But this ambition is misguided. The vast bulk of flesh has no potential for sprouting, it has congealed in the attempt and now just hangs there, grape-like clusters of hopeless blobs dangling from my person. A smile, or any attempt to lift this resigned flesh, only makes it swing. Protuberans, probolos, pondus, pinguis. Old Plinius. Where are my features? They are stuck in the motions of the flesh, its attempt to climb and all too sudden, all too pointy culmination, its piecemeal, flaccid defeat. If I were to interpret my face as it watches me and I watch it, it would be like this: a striving to raise unwilling flesh. A striving misguided from the outset. And so lies my face before me, caged in the mirror, and I, caged in the face, hidden from my sight, staring at the inevitable collapse; that is my face, and the balance between hope and defeat I inhabit. And I am like a murky mirror, caged in a face, now caged in a murky mirror. But as long as there are still openings to the world, there is hope. My worst nightmare, recurring since childhood: My face is terminally sealed and has no openings to the world. I am resigned to an inner world that can neither be sensed nor described. After fumbling for a long time, I find a sharp tool. I try to prick holes in the flesh, carve eye openings, nostrils, ears, mouth, but the knife, or whatever it is, only digs at the bonebed. The skull, the flesh encasing it, is sealed. In Germania, I have seen several soldiers have the top of their skulls drilled after a blow or a fall to ease the pressure of the amassed blood. Some died, some recovered. I have heard of people who lived for twenty, thirty years after such a procedure.

Sometimes I long for that opening. An opening in my head, not turned to the vile world of man but to the sky.

Pliny the Younger

Two days after the last day he had seen, his body was found intact and uninjured, still fully clothed and looking more like sleep than death. They dug him from the ash and layers of pumice covering him and made a wax imprint of his face. I have since had a mask cast in bronze from the model, and it hangs right here in front of me in my study. It is a calm and harmonious face, a face in peace with itself, having allowed itself to fall and sag. All the furrows of the face are deeper than he permitted them to be when he was alive. To claim it smiles peacefully would be an overstatement, but I sometimes find that the sunken jaw has an idiot grin pasted upon it. Not a grin directed at me or the world at large, but at something taking place only behind closed eyelids. And true peace, I believe, is not made apparent in the so-called peaceful smiles remaining on the lips of old men, dead after years of ills and anxiety. That kind of smile is full of resignation and expresses nothing but willing defeat. True peace is found in an idiot grin like the one I glimpse from time to time in the cast of my uncle's face. Calpurnia often asks me to have the face altered—have his eyes opened, his jaws lifted, his brows made to frown a bit—to make him seem awake and warlike. Possibly remove a few double chins and adorn the forehead with wavy locks in the style of Alexander. She finds it inappropriate to display one's ancestors in their dozy death rattle. But so far, I have resisted.

Quote, Naturalis Historia

That which the Earth buries and conceals in her depths, that which does not readily come to light, that is what kills us and drags us to the underworld.

Quote, Naturalis Historia

In Africa, I saw with my own eyes Lucius Constitius, a citizen of Thysdritum, who had turned into a man on her wedding day.

Pliny the Elder

He said: No one could have been more surprised than I. He said: I am the only woman who has ever raped herself from the inside. He said: No moment could have been more inconvenient. He said: I believe it was an all too powerful lust for my husband that made me become a man. He said: Of all my misfortunes, the most bitter is this, that in my misery I am named the happiest of women.

Quote, Naturalis Historia

Under the sun, the great star Venus revolves, shifting between alternate courses and rivaling the sun and the moon in names. When it rises before the sun it bears the name of Lucifer, as if it were another sun bringing forth the day, but when it shines after sunset it goes by the name of Vesper, prolonging the last light and performing the office of the moon. This trait of Venus was first discovered by Pythagoras of Samos around the 42nd Olympiad, that is the 142nd year of the founding of Rome. It is vaster than other stars as well and burns so brightly that it is the only star whose shine casts shadows. This explains the dispute over its name. Some have called it Juno, others Isis or the Mother of the Gods. Under its influence, all things on Earth are generated, for as Venus rises it drizzles a fertilizing dew that grants not only the Earth but all living things the power to conceive.

Diocles

The master has asked me to transcribe the story of my flight from the house two nights ago, and of my theft of a certain silver pitcher. The master says that a meticulous written account will assist him in choosing the appropriate punishment, and naturally I should be thankful I was not branded or crucified immediately. But since it was from writing I fled in the first place, the master must know it's a punishment in itself. The sores on my right hand, my writing hand, reopened long ago. The master lies in the dark next to me. He's wheezing. I don't know if he's sleeping or awake. Either way, his sleep is never deep. I fear he will interrupt me if I pause writing even for a moment, holler that it will do and ask to see my unfinished account on which he'll make his verdict. When the thought rests, the lie awakens, he always says. I do think it's best to get things down without notable hesitation. I'd come halfway down the slope with the silver pitcher in my hand, and felt compelled to set down a description of a nightmare that fell gently in flakes over the sea, even though I'm perfectly aware that poetic digressions will have no effect on the severity of my sentencing and probably won't illuminate anything anyway. But as it will be hard to describe, I'll allow myself these warm-ups. Acquaint myself with language and see if it will receive me. The poet's *licentia* is postulated, but the slave's is inborn, and he's expected to be chained to it. The masks portraying the faces of laughing slaves in plays, with big mouths that open and close and gape wide enough for the actors to stuff a whole chicken into while the audience cheers. The mock-cock that's bound around their waists. The witless grin and the erection. Not even as they conspire behind their master's back, or as the master beats them with a stick for their disobedience, do their grins fade or their wooden cocks falter. Is that not a kind of *licentia*? Never once in these theatrical farces do we hear the incensed master remark that the slave is still grinning, still lustful under his beating and humiliation. But now such an event has occurred. The master has become angry with his loyal scribe's foolish mask and costume cock, and the master doesn't understand that the scribe can do away with neither grin nor prick but has always been as chained to this *licentia* as he is presently chained to the bronze desk in the master's bedroom. Let me insert here that on my downhill course I tumbled and skidded until my right ankle got tangled on a tree root. It brought me to a halt so violent I screamed. I'd made a full turn to lay with my head downward so that I could see the villa above me. Here, I was tempted to say that I saw the villa towering above me, but the villa doesn't tower even though it's big, and the master has no doubt noticed as well. The villa shrinks into its own darkness up there. A short while later I couldn't feel the pain anymore, or any border between my leg and the tree. The sun was high in the sky, and I could see that the pitcher in my hand was ornamented with scenes depicting the fall of Troy. One side shows Aeneas catching a glimpse of Helen as she hides inside Vesta's temple. He looks vexed and grisly, sword in hand, like he's considering whether to end the bitch. On the other side, Pyrrhus hurls the small Astyanax over the city wall while Andromache the mother stands by and in despair claws her peachy cheeks till they bleed. I tried to recall a verse to do with some of it, but there's too much drivel in my head and too little beauty. It's the master's fault. It's his voice haunting me, cataloging every trivial detail of the world and fretting about all those details. The master's mapping of nature doesn't amount to anything, it only steeps the world in doubt and hesitation and tedious references to other authors' doubts and hesitations. How I'd love to recall a verse that was beautiful and brutal that I could have bellowed as I lay here, halfway between the villa and the town, but I only remembered the bilge and doubt and hesitation that I've been an instrument to for years. Me, I would have reacted differently to the sight of Helen cringing in the shadows of Vesta's temple with all of Troy ablaze around her. The morning star lets her lusty dew drip on the world and me. I lay there, head down, legs tangled in the tree roots. My prick became hard and through my entanglement I assume this cypress had its first erection too. This is the unity you have no part in. The morning star rouses the same urge in everybody, and everybody wants to move in the same direction, forward, upward, and inward. But you just stand and gape. You have no desire to fill the world with more life, you believe there's too much already, more than you can describe and name. I wish you could feel it from within, when the morning star's dew renders the world lustful, the feeling of sharing your instinct with the trees and the grass and the insects. Nature screams for cock and cunt. The smell of flowers and grass is far more obscene than the black soot spluttering from the hissing lamps in brothels. It's a willing scent. Don't you know that the stars are merely holes in the sky, through which the luminous ether can be seen at night? We came from ether and we'll return to it. It's what renders my sperm so shining and white. I aim my prick at Venus, the lustiest dew-dripping hole in the universe, and through me the trees and the grass and the earth fucked her, drenched in her cold morning juices. You were the only one who wasn't there, master.

Quote, Naturalis Historia

We are all at the mercy of chance to such a degree that chance itself—which in its essence casts doubt on the existence of any god—becomes a god.

Pliny the Elder

The worship of the blind goddess Fortuna is moving because it is so hopeless. What does it matter if you sacrifice a hundred oxen to fortune; how could it be anything but fortuitous? Fortuna is not only blind, she is sealed, her face has no orifices at all, which is why people make sacrifices to her with the greatest zest, anxiety and vigor. A sacrifice to Fortuna is never a mere technicality. She is courted for her incorruptibility. Everybody hopes that they alone can be her chosen one because they realize that no one else can be. Nonius, a tradesman of Novum Comum, pledged to build Fortuna an altar and pay homage with sizable offerings if he returned unscathed from a voyage to Bithynia. Everything worked out to his advantage. He made more than he'd dared to hope and owing to a favorable wind, he was swiftly reunited with his family. His first undertaking was to construct an altar on a small mound on the town outskirts. It was decorated with gold and silver and fine green marble. Mounted on top was a portrait of the goddess carved from an enormous piece of ivory, a gift from the proconsul, one of Nonius' chums whom he consistently called by his first name. Depicted here was not the blind goddess Fors Fortuna, but a young, beautiful and smiling goddess of good fortune carrying a horn of plenty in her arms. Four of the household's slaves guarded the altar day and night. When the day the priest had deemed most suitable for sacrifice arrived, the entire town gathered to witness Nonius carry out his promise. The young men and women had had their heads wreathed in flowers, and they were dancing around the mound hand in hand, singing praises. Nonius sacrificed fat geese, a white buck, a sow with piglets, incense, Egyptian salve. Unblended wine was splashed onto the altar and served generously to everyone present. Nonius stood hunched behind the sacrificial priest, gazing over his shoulder at the animals' guts while he alternately fidgeted with his signet ring or fingered one of his wig's golden curls. His grand manners of the previous months dwindled under his anxiety. But the priest assured him that the omens were good. Everyone cheered and old women had been hired to cry in relief. To complete the ceremony, Nonius along with his wife and children kneeled at the altar and thanked the goddess. Perhaps it was simply that the area's soil, soggy to begin with and now soupy with wine and blood and the whole town stomping around, could no longer support the altar. Or perhaps it was an earthquake, extremely limited in effect. None of us standing at the foot of the mound felt it, and the city was untouched.

Pliny the Younger

It is quite a pity that my uncle did not live to witness our mighty emperor Trajan, who is truly, and deservedly, Fortuna's favorite.

Pliny the Elder

It is said of Caesar the dictator that as a young man he dreamt he raped his mother. It was the same dream that ignited his ambition because he took it to mean that his mother was the Earth herself, and that he would one day become her master. To his mind the disgrace of the offense was entirely eclipsed by the fact that its achievement was within his *power*. It was Caesar who in his time—and with the characteristic contempt for divinity that ultimately led to his own deification—had the marsh drained where Novum Comum was founded. By doing so he ceded part of the goddess's realm to mortals with no sacrificial offerings or temple constructions to atone for the infraction. For naturally a goddess lived in the lake, and naturally she wasn't thrilled to see her realm diminished. Her true name was believed to be Laria but she was only ever called Coma Viridis, *greenhair*. The prior settlers, the Orobians, a Gaulish people, probably had closer ties to her, what do I know. They weren't here anymore, the remaining few had withdrawn to remote parts of the hills and didn't dare to approach the lakeshore. Each summer a wooden figure in the goddess's image, with hair of light green rushes and water lilies for breasts, was launched on a small raft. The figure was placed atop a pile of twigs and straw, which, once the raft had made some distance to the shore, was set alight by flaming arrows. The young townsmen competed in firing the shot that would engulf the pile in flames instantaneously. The winner would boast the title of the King of the Lake until the following year. The idea behind the ritual was never discussed but it must have been introduced with the intention of sending an annual message of warning to the lake's green-haired mistress. That she had better stay submerged and keep from meddling in human affairs. I imagined her supine body on the lakebed looking up at her burning portrait, hissing with anger though no emotion could be discerned in her dark pike eyes—the fire in them was merely the reflection of the flames on the surface. As the sun set and the portrait of the goddess burned, the King of the Lake would mate with a whore on the muddy bank while the town cheered and applauded, setting the beat of the mating with cymbals and rattles. She was painted green with rushes braided into her hair. I feared those whores as a boy. I remember how I squeezed between my mother's legs, and how my mother took my hands and clapped with them. I did not understand the meaning of it and I didn't understand the clamor and rejoicing, why the green woman screamed and howled. The only copulation I had witnessed had been between my father and my mother or one of the slaves, always a fully clad and silent affair under a blanket in the dining room before he retreated to his bedroom and my mother, or the slave, to theirs. After the mating, the green whore was required to take a swim in the lake to ensure the Lake King's insemination of the cruel goddess. It was assumed, I suppose, that she might render the lake barren were she not in this way mounted against her will and by proxy by the town's blooming youths. I remember two specimens from my childhood who were believed to be the products of this ritual. Both named Larius like the lake. They lived off the town and were not to be bothered. They were largely above the law and behaved accordingly. One of them was about my age, the other was a grown man with a cleft lip and an ailment known as silver skin because of the light skin that loosens and flakes from all over the sufferer's body. Despite sharing neither mother nor father they were regarded as brothers. They lived together in a little house by the banks, erected and granted to them by the town, and they were inseparable; one was rarely seen without the other's member inside his anus or his mouth. In the end, the younger Larius jabbed a knife into the throat of a traveling salesman who disagreed that everything was free of charge to the spawn of the goddess, and who wouldn't let him have a pouch of glass marbles without paying. At this, their joint list of offenses had exceeded the town's tolerance and it was deemed justifiable to kill them both. I remember how the useless brothers, who had never done a day's work in their lives, screamed for their mother as they stood on the raft and the flames began catching around them. Their last hope was the notion of motherly love in the greenhaired goddess who lay staring at them through her pike eyes on the bottom of her lake, hardly more stricken with grief at watching her progeny expire than at seeing a tadpole swallowed by a fish or a frog swept up in a heron's beak. They were all the children of the goddess, and she was equally disinterested in each of them. (In the same disinterested fashion nature watches our troubles with the suffering she has created for us. A cross-eyed gaze with the tongue nailed onto the forehead). That night the part of the goddess was played by a slave boy instead of a woman. He wasn't eager to bathe in the lake after copulating, fearing as he did the revenge of the goddess, and was threatened with a whip before he obeyed. He laughed nervously as he splashed about rinsing out the semen. It was the last time I attended the ritual, but my sister tells me it still takes place each year, with slave boys instead of women.

Pliny the Younger

A yearly celebration by the lakeshore does take place in Novum Comum, it is true, but the rest of the story is sheer folly. As a child, my uncle was surely frightened by some of the songs and dances performed at the festivities. I remember seeing a choir dance at such an occasion myself, they were clad in grass skirts and masks. Perhaps some older boys had been telling him a story or two. As is true of many gifted people, he was a little tense and impressionable throughout his life. Sophocles was scared stiff the few times he watched a performance of one of his own plays, but many prominent Roman minds also lacked in their youth the courage that would come to characterize the achievements of their maturity. One might easily compose a poem on the topic, but to whom should it be dedicated?

Quote, Naturalis Historia

A few things still need to be said about the world.

Quote, Naturalis Historia

The stars are attached to the firmament but contrary to common belief we are not allotted one each—according to an arrangement where brightly shining stars are supposedly for the rich, less bright stars are for the poor, and the very dim for invalids, with the allotment of light dished out in accordance with each individual's lot in life. The stars are not born coupled to humans either, and when a star shoots across the sky it is not a sign that a life has ended. No such great community exists between us and the heavens that would see starlight engage with our mortality.

Pliny the Younger

A few exceptions deserve mention, though. A bright new star was born in the sky upon the death of Caesar, and upon the enthronement of our mighty emperor Trajan a new star was observed, heralding the immortal glory awaiting him.

Quote, Naturalis Historia

Stars exist in the ocean and on land. I have seen stars form a halo around the javelins of soldiers who guard the camp at night, and I have seen stars descend on the yard and other parts of the ship and hop like birds from place to place with a sound reminiscent of voices.

Pliny the Younger

He is confusing stars with fireflies or something.

Quote, Naturalis Historia

Stars may be seen around people's heads at nighttime. The reason behind all this is unclear and lies hidden in the majesty of Nature.

Pliny the Elder

But it is beautiful.

Quote, Naturalis Historia

I have found twenty thousand topics worth consideration, most too obscure to have reached public attention, garnered from two thousand books or so—for, as Domitius Piso says, it is storage space not books we lack—written by a hundred authors whose work I have perused and augmented with insights that my predecessors did not possess, or were established after their time. I have no doubt that much has been omitted. For I am merely a man and duties consume my days, and my work must recede to my spare time, so don't think that I spend nights in repose.

Scene 4

Plinius lies on his back and stares into the dark. With his right-hand thumb and index finger he fondles a lock of hair on his forehead, starched with dried sweat. The room is sealed and the two lamps are issuing dark fumes. The air reeks of fat and soot, the bed is soggy with the sweat of fever, festering like a dung heap. The floor abounds with buckets of wood and leather containing piles of scrolls. Greek works with titles such as *The Horn of Plenty, The Riches of the Earth, The Flower Bouquet, Conversations by the Lamplight, Showers of Learning and Violets.* Shorter Latin works with dry titles: *Orations on Mining, Hand Book, Book of Excerpts, Nightly Words.* A slave boy reads aloud, an older slave takes notes after Plinius' directions. Some color has returned to

Plinius' cheeks, and the strain and whistle has eased a little from his breathing. His mood is terrible though. Damned Greeks, he screams so his throat squeaks. There's no end to their arrogance. There is no pit emptier than the ten books of Menecrates' *Horn of Plenty*, and you can't even imagine the stress I endured to obtain this botchwork. It had to be shipped from Alexandria! None of the slaves look Plinius in the eye while he's yelling, he's on his back, wide-open eyes turned ceilingward. The lamplight pulses, offering brief glimpses of the heavy ceiling stones. It appears as though the ceiling is heaving up and down to the rhythm of Plinius' labored breathing. Two stripes of gooey blood stream from his nostrils and meet in his philtrum where they form a joint stream that wells over quivering lips. Not a moment before the taste reaches his tongue, does he shout for powdered nettle root, wool and rose oil.

Quote, Naturalis Historia

If a mushroom grows near a serpent's nest, or if a serpent's breath touches a sprouting mushroom, it is possible for the mushroom—through its kinship with poison—to imbibe the poison. For this reason, one ought to be cautious of mushrooms when the serpent is not in hibernation.

Pliny the Elder

I am in a tavern in Ostia, having a bowl of beans. The host introduces me to his daughter who was born without orifices. He seats her on the bench next to me. Her face and neck are shrouded behind a veil of long, black hair. The host tells me she was born at the beginning of Nero's rule. Upon Nero's death, she uttered a rumbling sound for three days but the origin of the rumbling is not known. That's all she has ever done, he says, and many patrons travel to see her so I thought she might interest you. I put the bowl of beans back on the table and part her hair. No features are revealed underneath, only smooth, pale skin with freckles and the odd birthmark. In the absence of any true features, some of these marks come to take on a kind of symbolic meaning. By its shape and location one birthmark suggests a nostril which I must trace with a finger to confirm it is not an orifice. Still, it's hard not to think of it as a nostril. She has ears, well-shaped ears, but they are purely ornamental with no holes leading inside. I pull at the skin where the face ought to have been to establish that it is not a mask, skin tucked over a face. She tolerates it. Then I make her stand, push her gently to the middle of the floor and undress her. The host follows with a lamp to assist my investigation. She doesn't resist. She even raises her arms so that I may pull off her tunic. She must have been undressed in this manner before, and her sense of touch seems to be intact. She must be around seventeen by now if the host's words are to be trusted. She's a little on the skinny side, but her breasts and buttocks are full. I kneel in front of her and examine her lap in the lamp's glow. She has ordinary pubic hair and labias but no opening between them. She spins of her own accord and bends, parting her buttocks, seemingly in the habit of exhibiting her body from every angle. There is no rectal opening either. What is her nourishment, I ask the host and he explains that they put her outside when it rains and rub fat and oil into her skin every day, approximately where her cheeks should have been, a place marked by two roundish formations of freckles. Otherwise she shrinks, he says. I have never felt so much lust in my life, never felt so overcome with desire to seize something living, and I immediately ask him the price of taking her with me to my room. Three denarii, he says. And you may do with her as you wish, but you must let her skin breathe, and you mustn't prick holes. We had a fish sauce dealer who cut her, but there's no hole under the skin anyway so it's best not to. It's bad for business and it takes an age to heal, he says, flashing the apologetic smile typical of vendors explaining inconvenient but unavoidable pecuniary considerations. I promptly hand him the money and take his lamp. I drag the girl upstairs to my room, throw her on the bed, bolt the door, and place the lamp on the floor. I trail my cock all over her closed body, turn her this way and that way, pinch and pull at her breasts and buttocks and say: You're mine, I bought you. For hours, I toss around on top of her. When the lamp starts to flicker, I kneel and rub myself against her freckled cheek until I ejaculate, braying with pleasure. I remain sitting, watching with a sense of power and bewilderment as semen seeps into the skin of her cheeks. Then the light goes out. It is unlikely that a child will come of this intake of sperm, but should it come to pass it is hard to judge whether to allow it to remain inside her. Whether anyone could resist the urge to capture something so sequestered from the world.

Pliny the Younger

Gaius Plinius Caecilius Secundus greets his dear Cornelius Tacitus.

You respectfully decline to attend my poetry reading, and I believe I understand your reasons. Honestly, I too find these readings tiring, even if they are intended for a select circle of refined souls and hardly last longer than the afternoon. I do not wish to exhaust anyone with my delivery of poetic trifles, and to my credit I can now say that at least I will not be exhausting you, regardless of how the event unfolds. The unique aspect of this particular performance is that my wife Calpurnia intends to accompany me on her lyre hidden behind a curtain next to the podium as though the music streams from the very poems. The curtain is adorned with a mountainous landscape, complete with shepherds and sheep, with silens and a merry Bacchus right at the center of the circle. The overall impression, as I read my poems to the music streaming from Arcadia, is charming, if I may say so, and I say it knowing that charm alone will not be enough for you. Calpurnia has never received any formal musical training, it is her love for my poetry alone that compels her to play the lyre. Viewed from this perspective, I find it rather reassuring that an artist of your caliber will not be seated among the audience. I was practically forced to extend an invitation to you as my dear Calpurnia is convinced that her love is enough to excuse all technical shortcomings and render the show palatable to even the most refined taste buds. How sorry she will be when I tell her that you are prevented from attending! But she will swiftly turn her regret into bitterness, and there will hardly be a slave girl or matron left untouched by this reaction. You know me well enough to trust that my heart is not burdened in the least by it. You surely have weightier matters to attend to, as you and I both know, and it is your importance in particular that sparks the sputter of resentment from my Calpurnia, which seems to be reaching my ears already.

Furthermore you ask me why I have built an auditorium in my villa, and why I would waste my own and other people's time delivering poems that I freely admit have cost me no trouble worth noting. Had these questions been posed by a lesser man, I would have considered them cheeky. But since it is you, prodding at my vanity, I must find a way to let vanity answer for itself.

I will agree with you insofar that vanity should not guide one's path through life. Concurrently, I am unable to think of a single great man who has not let his vanity do exactly that. Let us quickly agree that Emperor Claudius and his successor Nero, as well as Nero's bald epigone Domitian, all embarrassed themselves in their itch for recognition through hourlong readings. But the urge to impress the cultivated public with poetry was found in Cicero as well, in the Divine Julius, and—closer to our time—in Seneca. Even as the latter sat on Nero's back as comfortably as the farmer on his donkey, he never ceased braying himself.

Even more, I can inform you that the urge compelled my uncle as well, and pay heed to this, my dear Tacitus, as we both know how your own work has benefited greatly from his historical writing, his books on Germania and rhetoric. Naturally, it is to your merit that you have no craving for the immediate recognition that may be achieved at a reading. Mostly because your work would not really stir an audience anyway. To obtain success with a reading, each sentence must spark the imagination of even the most lethargic listener. Should you wish to thrill an audience with a pastoral poem, Arcadia must be evoked in brazen colors, not as a foggy silhouette of idyll. In the genre's every sentence the listener must find a tranquil spot to rest his head or an image drawing a covetous sigh. Your own historical writings, which you call impartial, are nuanced to such an extent that they cannot be loved. You are wise to avoid confrontation with the fact. Unadorned prose has no place in an auditorium crammed full of senators and equites dressed in their finery.

As a boy I stood behind the curtain and listened to my uncle read from his Natural History in Emperor Vespasian's summer home at Baiae. It was not my uncle's wish to perform, although he had been quick to yield. He had never read from his scientific works in public and I doubt that the busy Vespasian had so much as glanced at this work, all he knew was that my uncle was a prolific writer with no audience, and since he was very fond of him, he wished to do him a service by arranging for a reading to be held at his villa. Of course, he must have expected my uncle—being a man of great talents—to impress the discerning minds in attendance and cast a glow of literary refinement on his court. The greatest men of the time were gathered. Word was, my uncle would read from a book on flowers, and so the auditorium was decorated with an abundance of flowers; the floor was overspread with petals and under each bench lay fragrant bouquets. The podium itself was completely covered with roses and peonies, and through holes in the ceiling, slaves released dried buds and leaves by the handfuls which gathered in the folds of the assembled togas. Wreaths of vine and flowers were shared among the audience, as well as cups containing a liquid that I believe was rose wine; probably something the emperor had brought home from a campaign and saved for a special occasion. As the audience bustled inside, my uncle stood behind the curtain with my mother and me, peering anxiously out. He was clutching the papyrus scroll tightly under his left arm, and each time another official, poet, or man of wealth stepped inside, received his wreath and his cup of wine and settled into his seat, my uncle squeezed my hand tightly and sighed. When the room was full and the doors shut, he emerged from behind the curtain. He was dressed in a colorful toga and the wreath of flowers around his head was gilded. The applause was extraordinary as you might imagine for a reading arranged by the emperor. Before it had tapered off my uncle suffered his first bout of panic. There was no chair on the podium and my uncle needed a chair, he could not read standing. A slave arrived with a chair for him and he let his large body sink deeply into it. He was barely visible to the audience behind the enormous flower arrangement. Also, I could see that his breathing had become troubled. As you know, he suffered from shortness of breath and the incredible number of flowers thickened the air to a soup, sweet and sticky like honey. Wheezing and hiccupping he thanked the audience, whom he could no longer see, and who could no longer see him over the hedge of pink peonies. Then he commenced reading from the thirteenth book of his Natural History, a mix of oldish wrath against the use of perfumes and dry listings of ingredients and trade routes. Before an audience of men who had just spent their entire morning having their bodies rubbed in exotic balms he now ventured forth in his feeble, hissing voice. "Lucius Plotius—brother of censor and twice consul, Lucius Plancius—was discovered at his hiding place in Salernum by the pungent waft of his balm after the triumvirate had proscribed him; and this disgrace indeed justifies his proscription, for who would not share the opinion that such men deserve to be killed?"

Had the emperor not been sitting in the first row, emitting such strong, exotic fragrances himself, the poor perfumed men would have believed the reading had been arranged with the sole purpose of mocking them.

He paused once, midway through a description of varied palms and dates (because, as you know, the thirteenth book is about much more than flowers) and asked for something to drink. His voice was softer than my mother's, softer than my own boy's voice, and the words were squeezed out laboriously in stubborn little bursts. He was given a cup of rose wine and took a great draught upon which his throat constricted and the rose wine spurted from his nose and mouth, seeped down neck and toga and onto the papyrus in front of him.

He managed to read for about an hour in the sickly-sweet soup atmosphere before he started gasping and clutched his neck and the blood began pouring from his nose. Then he fell out of the chair, and if his assistant had not quickly swept him offstage with the help of a few imperial life guards, it would have been the embezzlements on the Earth's surface, not her burning belly, that would have ended him.

When I tell you this story it is mostly to advise you against reading to an audience yourself. I know you respect my uncle's work profoundly since you treat it with the same reverence

Egyptians reserve for their dead kings (first the brain is extracted with a hook, then the body is drained of liquid and lastly you stand with a withered bundle, dedicated to all of posterity). By his performance, my uncle fell out of the emperor's good graces, fell out with all who walked and breathed in decent society. When the emperor later made him admiral of the fleet at Misenum it was mostly to get him out of town—had it not been for the unfortunate reading, greater positions had likely been in store for him. I have drawn my own lessons and write therefore only with the modern audience in mind, and not to endorse some expired ideal of acorn-munching peasants as particularly virtuous. Time will show whose vanity is greatest, yours or mine, Tacitus. Good luck with it all.

Pliny the Elder

I am sitting on a chair in my garden, it is morning. I have not slept. At brief intervals, my vision darkens, sleep pulls at me from within but I straighten my spine and breathe deeply, keeping my eyes open. The boy dabs my forehead with cold water, it helps. And the cool blade he now starts to scrape over my skin helps too. Between periods of blackness, formations of colored spots appear before my eyes. Or bubbles, rather, they froth, pop and disappear. A survey of the colors that appear before the exhausted eye, I dictate. The exhausted eye shuts tightly around the image of the world which it has absorbed, thereby blotting the vision with colors that have no origin in the world. Are the colors created by a liquid stored in the eye? The clamped, exhausted eye can't keep back the secretion of liquid, color accidentally spatters; drops that should have been stored in the eye for later visualizations. Bring me a rose, I shout. The redundant color spots have danced before my eyes for hours now. Could some of the juice needed for color representation have been depleted? Will the rose appear more pallid than before, or will it appear speckled in colorless dots now that the tired eye has squandered its juice prematurely? The master must sit still while I shave him, says the boy, and I clutch the armrests tightly with both hands. Could it be that the slime amassing in the corner of my eyes during sleep is truly congealed color juice, expelled as the eyes were painting my nightly dreams, I dictate. Investigate correlation between dreamlife and the eye's slime secretion. I sit without stirring for a little while, and he scrapes the blade across my left cheek. Lifelike dreams, I say. The blade makes a gash in my cheek, I can feel it, hear it even, steel slicing flesh. He gasps and pulls back the knife, I must be bleeding profusely, the blade is slick with blood. My cheek throbs, I feel the hot blood dripping down my neck. I seize his wrist, prise the knife from him. Spare me, says the boy, he raises both arms over his head, recoils. I bend over the bloody knife. The blood is dark, the red seems as saturated as always. I have seen much blood. No colorless spots appear in this portion, everything is as it should be, calm and inexplicable. Lifelike dreams followed by intense nightly slime secretion in the corners of the eyes may cause the colors of the real world to pale in the eye's impression, I dictate. The strong redness occupying my vision makes me doubt the idea, therefore the insertion of the word *may*.

Quote, Naturalis Historia

I have no doubt that much has been omitted. For I am merely a man and duties consume my days, and my work must recede to my spare time, so don't think that I spend nights in repose. The days I spend in your service, sleeping only what bare minimum my health requires, contenting myself with the one reward that while my time is spent on trifles (as remarked by Marcus Varro), I am adding hours to my life: for living only means to be awake.

Quote, Naturalis Historia

I myself have seen Arellius Fuscus—who was ousted from the equestrian order on a ludicrous, false charge —wearing rings of silver because of the hordes of young students that were attracted by his fame.

Pliny the Elder

And I have seen Arellius Fuscus calmly take a seat, slip the rings off both hands and place them in his lap to wipe them clean of blood in his cape, one by one, while his students that were still standing waved their arms theatrically and recited Demosthenes in unison.

Quote, Naturalis Historia

Formerly it was custom to wear rings on a single finger only; the one next to the little finger, as evidenced by statues of Numa and Servius Tullius. Later, the finger closest to the thumb was dressed in rings as well, and later again, the little finger. The peoples of Gallia and Britannia are said to wear rings on the middle finger, whereas here this finger alone is spared; the others must carry the load and each joint gets its own little ring.

Pliny the Elder

He used to slap them, backhand in severe cases. The silver
flared through the air, ripping up the plump young cheeks with
signet stones and curlicues.

Quote, Naturalis Historia

Man is the only animal to experience shame after his first mating; a clear sign that the origin of life is shameful. Other animals mate during a fixed period each year, humans do it anytime, night or day. In animals, there are limits to the desire for mating, whereas in humans there seems to be none.

Pliny the Elder

We moved to Rome when I was eleven. We lived in an apartment on the Quirinal for seven years, my father's shop faced the street and the apartment was on the first floor. Across from us lay a spice depot and a strong waft of cinnamon, cardamom and ginger somewhat dulcified the stench of the city. My father offered loans to freedmen and employed a couple of redeemed gladiators to collect the debts. They lived one floor up. If the loans were not repaid, my father took the debtor's property. The gladiators came calling clad in their old armor, which was not exactly practical but highly intimidating. A Samnite, heavily armed, and a retiarius. I always imagined the retiarius catching the debtors in his net as they tried to make a run for it down the crowded alleys of Subura or Transtiberim. How they'd wriggle and plead with exotic gods in their broken tongues as my father leaned over them, flushed, threatening them with slow and painful deaths.

I went to the school of Arellius Fuscus. I could recite the Law of the Twelve Tables in my sleep, *Whoever enchants away crops be damned, damned be the sorcerer.* When my father's business associates came by, I recited Homer or spun orations from any word they suggested. Sobbing on my knees, I maintained Helen's innocence, or pleaded to the best of my ability for the pardon of Astyanax, the young son of Hector. I iterated in fifty ways the tale of Solon and Croesus and my father's friends rewarded me with coins and nuts and marbles for my efforts.

When at the age of fourteen I was to receive my first toga, they sent for Lalagia, our slave girl. A cross-eyed, nervous woman, whom I believe my father chose for the purpose because she was familiar and experienced. She traveled all the way from Novum Comum to vent the pressure I was presumed to experience and prevent it from leading me in some unfortunate direction—such as an infatuation with a freeborn who might distract me from my studies.

To begin with, my father showed me how it was done. So there I was, in my new white toga, gawking at his clenched buttocks in the light of the lamp she was holding, her arm stretched out away from him to prevent the oil from splattering on the master. Afterward she tried without success to coax my own erection. She tugged and pulled at me with her legs spread wide, a stripe of my father's semen dripping from her lap. All it made me think of was her son. He was a little younger than I and he had been attending my school lectures since I was seven. Her scoliotic son with the scarred face who now lived in the upstairs chamber with the two gladiators, and who each morning on our way to school (where his wounds would inevitably be ripped open afresh by the clusters of silver rings hurled at his face and body), bragged about all the whores he fucked with the gladiators upstairs. Last night, she was Syrian; last night she was Jewish; last night she was Gaetuli, and I fucked her fat black ass until she screamed (we skipped along between the stones in the alley to avoid soiling our sandals in the shit and piss emptied out of the windows at night, chewing lupine seeds or a slab of bread. At this hour, the streets were predominantly trod by heavily loaded slaves and clients rushing to bring routine morning greetings to their respective benefactors, already arranging their faces in suitably humble grimaces. Our sandals clicked on the half-empty streets as the birdsong blended with Diocles' bragging. These mornings were the highlights of my days for many years).

But I knew he lied. No woman ever entered the house, my father wouldn't allow it. Whatever gasps and moans sank through the floorboards could only have come from the gladiators and the boy. That I should be lying downstairs astride his mother, whose arrival had actually made him lift his head up, appeared to me quite unjust. That we eventually succeeded is only due to an exertion of willpower on my part, mostly because I didn't want her to be punished for the failed attempts.

Only once did I tell him on our way to school. I couldn't stand listening to the slave's unseemly bragging anymore. I closed my eyes, placed my palm on my chest where the golden orb was no longer hanging, and said; Last night, it was your mother. I remained standing like that, awaiting the slap that never came.

Quote, Naturalis Historia

It is broadly agreed upon—and there is nothing I would more readily believe—that sorcerers (who are certainly swindlers, that much is clear) will have their enchantments impeded by the least smear of menstrual blood on their doorposts.

Scene 5

Here comes Rectina, clopping bowlegged up the slope to Plinius' villa. She has to lean on a stick made of polished African citron tree with a handle carved like a horse's head and a silver-plated tip. It's all the births that have skewed her legs like that, when she huffs and heaves it doesn't sound like exertion so much as sacrifice even if no one can hear her panting right now. The thick smears of lead-white and cinnabar on her face are already smudged and glossy with sweat. In her left hand, she's carrying a basket crammed with honey bread and soft cheese in small clay jars all covered by a wool blanket of her own making.

—You ought to take better care of yourself, she says once she has taken a seat by Plinius' bed.—You can't trust the slaves with everything. How long did they leave you there? She has pulled the chair up next to his bed and she's hunching slightly over him. The wool blanket is folded over her knee, in a moment she is going to tuck it around him.

Rectina's stela might say, at best:

81

DAUGHTER OF MANIUS RECTINUS MAEROR

OF THE EQUESTRIAN ORDER

MOTHER OF EIGHT

LOYAL WIFE

SPUN WOOL

and possibly:

TREAD LIGHTLY, STRANGER

But who would commission such a stela? The children's father is long dead (he died after prolonged illness, which made him weak and whiny but didn't stop him, shivering with fever, from impregnating her one last time), the sons have left and the youngest daughter is happily married. The last time some offshoot or other paid her a visit, she clearly sensed the objective was to evaluate her property, her fortune, and her health, which is all right, thanks for asking, except the little assholes forgot to close the gates to the world when they entered it and left her legs gaping for the remainder of her days.

There are still streaks of dried blood on Plinius' left chin. Without thinking, Rectina sucks on her thumb and wipes off the blood with it. Plinius doesn't jerk his head to evade her motherly reflex. He lies still and stares at the ceiling.

—I could cut your hair, she said. She also says, I can make wool softer than what's sticking out your nose right now. I'll see to it you have a decoction of thistle brought over to lower your fever, no wait, I'll bring it myself.

If it wasn't for Plinius' ailing state, he might've exploited the moment when Rectina rose to tuck him in with the blanket.

82

There are little things that only a mother or a wife would think to do. A free woman. The need for care and tenderness can't be satisfied by slaves alone. But Plinius' decline, his wispy locks, stiff with sweat, scream to Rectina that her presence is unwelcome despite Plinius' only sounds being small grunts of gratitude. Rectina's own hair is painstakingly, painfully, done up following the current fashion: Artificial poodle curls ridged high in front, framing her face from ear to ear, and a shoal of tight braids running behind it, tucked into a mussel-shaped, gold-netted bun at her nape. Having already spent hours personally preparing cakes, she then had to spend another few hours under the ornatrix's hands having her hair fixed with glowing irons, pin at the ready to poke the clumsy girl's arm if necessary. All this simply to play the role of good neighbor today.

Had Plinius known he harbored such a longing, the longing for a woman's tenderness—or that he could have had it—he might have kissed Rectina's forehead under the towering ridge of hair, right at the moment when Rectina tucked the blanket under his shoulders.

She sits back and looks at the woolly, grunting larva she has made out of the feverish man. Then she gets up, grabs her stick and hobbles home. Plinius wrests his right hand out from under the blanket only to find he has no use for it. He rolls the fringe of the blanket between his thumb and index finger. So he lies until darkness falls, and for once he sleeps through the night.

Pliny the Elder

Nature grants everyone an equal enemy. In her private amphitheater, she's the only audience to watch the games unfold. The
snake sucks the elephant's blood through a bite behind the ear
where the elephant's trunk cannot reach to fend it off—only
to expire under the weight of the drained elephant's carcass
when it collapses. Game over, both die, nature marvels at her
own ingenuity. She allows her mightiest predators to be slain by
cripples, like when the invalid Emperor Claudius killed a whale
in Ostia's harbor, or when her proudest creations—emperors,
generals, poets—fall prey to trivialities. Choked on a bite of as-
paragus, felled by a roof tile, stung by a bee inside the mouth.
Nature begets monsters, fire-breathing bulls with lion's teeth
who imitate human speech and call our names to lure us from
our tents and cabins. She created man solely so he could suffer,
the only animal who cries, the only animal who knows death
and understands the scope of its suffering. The only animal
who understands that it is made to suffer for nature's amuse-
ment. He who believes himself meant for bigger things is the
unknowing victim of nature's game, hardly better than an animal. My suggestion: We must learn to enjoy the cruel game, and
so be it that it is at our own expense. Learn each of the varied
malformations she may inflict on us, relish the endless kinds
of miseries imparted daily by her creativity. In spite and awe,
we must name her nefarious inventions. Let us see if we can
outlaugh the wailing, or even drown her mirth in our own. I

have collected twenty thousand examples of nature's sublime cruelty. Dear compatriots, you'd better start laughing now.

Quote, Naturalis Historia

An orca turned up at the port of Ostia and Emperor Claudius battled it. It arrived while he was constructing the harbor, attracted by a shipwreck carrying hides from Gaul. After gorging on the hides for days, it had managed to sink itself into a shallow seabed where the waves broke too high for it to turn. As it pursued its prey, led shoreward by the waves, its back rose above the surface like the keel of a capsized ship. On the Emperor's command nets were extended between the harbor inlets while he set out with the Praetorian Guard to give the people of Rome a show. Soldiers launched their harpoons as their boats flung by, and I saw one of the boats sink, drowned by water spewed forth by the monster.

Pliny the Elder

I am lying on my stomach on a blanket outside the villa, baking under the sun. My sister's boy, little Gaius, is wobbling around me. He is making a speech he has prepared in which he appeals to Lucretia not to take her own life after her rape by Tarquinius. I am lying here sweating, listening to a child tackle the elastics of guilt. It is part comforting and part alarming to hear him weigh the notion as deftly as any lawyer in the Forum. He is already indifferent. I can no longer feel the border between my body and the world, the hot blanket, the warm air. When I lie here, eyes closed, I feel borderless. The birds sing in me, the boy, with his hypocrite talk and theatrical gesticulation, walks in me. The tall plane tree, thronged by cicadas, snaps and hisses. I lie in the sun with my eyes closed, watching the illuminated insides of my lids. Warm red. In Germania I saw a king sacrifice a bull to his gods. The bull's blood was collected in a silver basin on an altar of turf. When the basin was full, the king placed a thin wooden disc on the surface. A face had been cut into both sides of the disc. One was angry and warlike, the other was laughing, tongue snaking from the open mouth. The disc trembled in the steaming blood with the laughing face up. Then the king placed the bull's testicles on the disc, which sank under their weight before popping back up, now with the angry warface on top. An omen, I believe. I feel like that face now, the laughing one, as it turned toward the bottom.

Scene 6

Diocles sleeps in his chair, curled over the bronze table he's chained to. He snores. The tablets with his written accounts are no longer in front of him. He wakes up as the caretaker Echion pulls the chair from under him and plants a knee on his belly, the next second crushing his left shin with an iron club. After a swift and hopeless struggle, Echion binds Diocles' wrists with a long rope. Come on, come on, come on, I have to tie you up, Echion mutters. Echion's hands are large and freckled with a tide of red curls along the edges. His hands are used to getting dirty. Once Diocles is bound, Echion unlocks his fetters and drags him off by rope, through the dark corridor and past the kitchen, latrine and winter dining room to the atrium where the noon sun falls through the roof opening where every slave in the house is gathered to witness the penalty for escape. Here, in the strong sunshine by the impluvium, almost blinded by its glistening water, the caretaker breaks Diocles' right leg after a few failed attempts (come on, lie still, I have to break your leg). He throws the club so it clinks on the tiles. Diocles screams shrilly, it sounds like fear more than pain. The new kitchen maid sobs, eyes pressed shut and hands covering her ears. Echion strokes her hair, then flings her hands down and says viewing is not optional. He'll visit her tonight, no matter what she says, whether or not her sign is still up. Now he drags the scrawny scribe off by the rope again. On through the house, along the next corridor, past guest rooms, wardrobe, house altar, tablinum, and out the open door where the harsh sunlight is flooding in. Three of Plinius' freedmen await them outside, sour-faced and cross-armed. It's their job to get Diocles up into the fig tree to the left of the door. Two of them lift him while the third throws the rope over a sturdy branch to hoist him up from the other side. They moan and grunt in the heat. The third climbs a couple of steps up the ladder while the other two lift the squirming Diocles. He ties the rope around the branch, fastening it so Diocles dangles just above ground. They've been instructed to hang him at eye level. Echion nails his feet to each side of the tree trunk, long nails going sideways through the ankles, behind the Achilles tendon. Under the head of each nail, small acacia planks are fastened preventing him from wrenching his feet off the nails. Overripe figs fall as Echion hammers, one of the freedmen lets out an accidental chuckle as a moldy fig bursts between the wisps of red on Echion's scalp. Echion raises his bloodstained face at him and bares his teeth.

Quote, Naturalis Historia

What I have attempted to describe in this work—the mutually attractive and repellent forces of nature, which the Greek have termed sympathy and antipathy—cannot be illuminated with a better example than this: That the invincible diamond, indifferent to iron and fire, nature's most violent powers, is broken asunder by goat's blood.

Pliny the Elder

The goat is a shameless mix of idiotic urges, garnished with the same elongated bristles that Greek sages proudly grew on their chins. It is worth observing that this ludicrous animal, the ever-libidinous, all-devouring buck named tragos by the Greek, has given a name to the dramatic portrayal of human suffering and destiny's relentlessness. Nothing exists in our world that is not infused with a drop of goat's blood.

Quote, Naturalis Historia

Who hatched the idea for this experiment, or by what coincidence was it discovered? Why would anyone suddenly wish to test the resilience of such an immensely prized object against the world's lowliest animal? Such discoveries and learnings must originate from the divine. Do not seek sense in nature, there is only will.

Pliny the Elder

The goat's yellow bubble-eye, striped with black down the middle, has no capacity for emotion, not at the time of death nor during their mating which the buck so zestfully pursues. A pig or a dog appears expressive next to a goat. Emperor Tiberius was called a goat because of his libido, naturally, but among our tyrants, his character appears the most unfathomable and contradictory as well. After that drop of goat's blood a pig mounted the throne and was superseded by a scabby dog. The dog was deified and calamities abounded. The blood of twenty legions cannot wash away the drop left behind by one goat.

Quote, Naturalis Historia

There are many considerations regarding the exterior likeness between humans, much of which is believed to be accidental; remembrances of sounds, visions or impressions occurring during the act of conception. Thoughts flashing in the minds of both participants are believed to influence whom the child will resemble, or to shuffle the features of the pair into new formations. Thus, a greater number of distinguishing features exist among men than among the individuals of any other species; because the quickness of human thought, his bright mind and individually unique character leave many outer marks. The other animals have dull minds and within their species they look a lot like each other.

Pliny the Elder

It should come as no surprise that the master's acumen seldom appears in his slaveborn children considering the circumstances usually characterizing such conceptions. A slave girl who knows to slink and wriggle in order to enhance the master's pleasure so that she may sooner return to her other duties will flush his mind and clear it of sober thoughts to such an extent that the progeny will turn out accordingly tubby. Unlike the child bred in a freeborn wife whose sole contribution to the coupling is to submit to his embrace, lovingly mindful of his accolades on the battlefield and in the forum, and whose belly receives his seed like a type of distinction. Whenever coitus with slave girls is performed with an addition to the household in mind, one ought to demand that she refrain from horny wriggling, that she instead lie still and think of something dignified. On such occasions it comes in useful to have memorized the Law of the Twelve Tables.

A tentative comparison between the slave's face and my own reveals certain shared traits that I've never given much thought before this moment as I hold his wax imprint in my hands. He lacks my noblest features though, such as the arc of the nose and the shapely lips that were passed down to both Plinia and me from our father, and which I envisage so vividly in little Gaius. The slave's marked cheekbones, prominent chin and close-set eyes give the air of brutal greed whose origin I fully understand as I too in my youth have sighed and moaned at his mother's expertly whorish regime. While my own face strives in vain to be lifted, freighted by the natural droop of flesh and fat, his face sets a steady course ahead. The nose is long and pointed, cleaved at the tip and thus cementing its likeness to a penis. Chin and forehead likewise shoot forth. Were one to follow their trajectory, from top and bottom, the face would inescapably meet itself—smacking shut like a set of writing tablets—in a helpless, rushed attempt to stride ahead. The cheeks are somewhat sunken, but the eyes are protruding and close-set as in all predators. Even in death, the lips are pursed as if leaning in for a kiss.

Pliny the Younger

For exactly this reason, I believe, Calpurnia never fails to arouse me when she reads from my uncle's works to me. The thought of the gifted children these moments might beget instils in me a sort of lust driven by reason.

Quote, Naturalis Historia

Some take a fragment of a nail or a bit of rope used for crucifixion, wrap it in wool and wear it around their neck against the quartan fever. After the patient has recovered, they hide it in a hole where the sunshine can't touch it.

Scene 7

Plinius has a nosebleed. He's lying on his back on the bed, staring into the dark. It's the older slave now hurrying to bring his tray of remedies. The boy hasn't stopped reading from Menecrates' *Horn of Plenty*, and Plinius hasn't ceased his resentful stream of comments on the work. In his right hand he's clutching the wool-wrapped nail on his chest and he's pressing his left palm against the moist, cold stones of the wall. The old man sits down on the side of the bed. Carefully, he dusts powdered nettle root in each of Plinius' nostrils with a silver spatula. His hands tremble, a portion misses and blends with the snot and blood on his lip. Then he wraps the small flakes of bark from the fig tree in wool, dips them in rose oil and softly inserts them into Plinius' nose. He places the tray at the foot of the bed, between two worn leather buckets full of scrolls, marked in chalk: *Catonis* and *Maronis*.

Quote, Naturalis Historia

Lust was born, life has ceased.

Scene 8

Plinius lies on his stomach, the sun rises. His chest has sunken into the pool of blood and urine. A bit of grimy blood still trickles from his nose. A group of boys scream and laugh, jostling through the necropolis and along the coast on their route to the sea for a morning dip. It sounds as though they're screaming: Long live the Emperor, father of the fatherland. Plinius has now registered the light whimper he emitted a moment ago and has adjusted to a deeper rattle. Under his furthermost chin he feels warm urine, and takes in the stench of fungus, rot and iron. He's cold and nauseous but he can breathe all right now, and even if the stench worsens he takes the air all the way in. Easy now, he mumbles through his right mouth corner, the one not touching the pool. The cocks and dogs down by the coast are attempting to scare off the new day with their clamor. Plinius tries to hoist himself up on his hands, but they slip and skid, it's impossible to find any balance. At last his left hand catches the trunk of the fig tree. After groping around the trunk for some time he finally finds the hole where a thick nail was recently removed. The tip of his thumb can go inside with a bit of effort. The other fingers he folds around the trunk, that way he's able to lift himself up a little. He moves his right hand to the side so that it supports his weight. He's standing on his knees now, a thick jet of vomit is ejected from his mouth and nose, he trembles and whimpers between bursts. *Eheu*, he says. He's on his legs now, they wobble under him. He stands for a moment to gather his courage, glaring in confusion and offense at the glistening ghastliness that collected in the spot where his body was thrashing just moments ago. His tunic is drenched and his face is grimy with piss, mud, blood and vomit. Now he screams for the slaves.

Quote, Naturalis Historia

Greetings, Nature, mother of all things, and deign to give me your favor, I am alone among Romans in praising you in your every expression.

Scene 9

Plinius wakes up in the dark. Moisture that has condensed on the ceiling is dripping on his face. Further east they're quarrying stones for a new road to Rome. The road will end where Nero's artificial lake used to be, between the Palatine, Esquiline and Caelius. In painful wheezes, the world is wrung from Plinius' fat neck in the dark. Diocles takes note, the stylus scribbles into the grubby wax. Once the road has been built, enormous boulders are cut out and hauled. By the end of the road, Emperor Vespasian is building his amphitheater. Presently, it looks like a cocoon, a maze of scaffolds, ramps, and treadmill cranes wound about its insides. The grinding, squeaking ropes and coils and pulleys, the moans and wails and lashing whips. Already, hundreds have died. In the end, it looks like a marble nest. On the perimeter are small booths with women and children from all over the world. You can pull back a curtain and fuck them in relative discretion, should the bloodbath in the arena have roused your desires. Outside of the booths, the animals from the day's fights are roasted, folks gnaw at slabs of meat from rhinos and elephants as well as the tigers and bears who, before their deaths, sated their hunger on human flesh. Split, clean bones are strewn everywhere. Plinius lies on his back and stares into the dark. He describes the universe, the stars, the planets, sun, moon, earth, its lands, mountains, forests, marshes, seas, lakes, rivers, isles, deserts, peoples, monsters, man, animals on the ground, animals in the sea, birds, insects, anatomy, physiognomy, trees, winemaking, flowers, fruits, herbs, plant-based remedies, remedies made from animal and human bodies, sorcery, rocks, mining, metals, minerals, art, precious stones. Had the chapters on art been the final, you might say man's triumph over nature had been the conclusion. But it's the book on precious stones that concludes the work. Plinius writes that no other citizen of Rome has described nature in all her aspects, and that he therefore hopes she will favor him. He has a nosebleed. Diocles dusts nettle root into his nostrils and stuffs them with wool soaked in rose oil. An enormous machine is switched on to chase down people and animals from all over the world to be slaughtered in Vespasian's amphitheater. All the knowledge needed to keep the machine running is contained in Plinius' Natural History. The world is big, and they've set about clearing it of beasts and barbarians. Everybody is invited to watch it unfold. Plinius publishes his Natural History, an attempt to master nature. He names nature the evil stepmother of man. Plinius is Vespasian's personal advisor in these years. Vespasian's attempt to master nature is more successful than Plinius', but Vespasian dies before the Colosseum, his amphitheater, is finished. Plinius erects his own monument in time. He dedicates it to Vespasian's son Titus. Then he dies in a natural disaster. Even on the days when Plinius lifts the shutters from the window hole in his room, the light doesn't reach the ceiling stones. They're clammy, covered in moss and soot. A drop falls on his tongue as he dictates, staring into the dark.

Appendix

Two Letters from Pliny the Younger

(translated by Betty Radice)

To Baebius Macer (Book Three, 5)

I am delighted to hear that your close study of my uncle's books has made you wish to possess them all. Since you ask me for a complete list, I will provide a bibliography, and arrange it in chronological order, for this is the sort of information also likely to please scholars.

Throwing the Javelin from Horseback—one volume; a work of industry and talent, written when he was a junior officer in the cavalry.

The Life of Pomponius Secundus—two volumes. My uncle was greatly loved by him and felt he owed this homage to his friend's memory.

The German Wars—twenty volumes, covering all the wars we have ever had with the Germans. He began this during his military service in Germany, as the result of a dream; in his sleep he saw standing over him the ghost of Drusus Nero, who had triumphed far and wide in Germany and died there. He committed his memory to my uncle's care, begging him to save him from the injustice of oblivion.

The Scholar—three volumes divided into six sections on account of their length, in which he trains the orator from his cradle and brings him to perfection.

Problems in Grammar—eight volumes; this he wrote during Nero's last years when the slavery of the times made it dangerous to write anything at all independent or inspired.

A Continuation of the History of Aufidius Bassus—thirty-one volumes.

A Natural History—thirty-seven volumes, a learned and comprehensive work as full of variety as nature itself.

You may wonder how such a busy man was able to complete so many volumes, many of them involving detailed study; and wonder still more when you learn that up to a certain age he practised at the bar, that he died at the age of fifty-five, and throughout the intervening years his time was much taken up with the important offices he held and his friendship with the Emperors. But he combined a penetrating intellect with amazing powers of concentration and the capacity to manage with the minimum of sleep.

From the feast of Vulcan onwards he began to work by lamplight, not with any idea of making a propitious start but to give himself more time for study, and would rise half-way through the night; in winter it would often be at midnight or an hour later, and two at the latest. Admittedly he fell asleep very easily, and would often doze and wake up again during his work. Before daybreak he would visit the Emperor Vespasian (who also made use of his nights) and then go to attend his official duties. On returning home, he devoted any spare time to his work. After something to eat (his meals during the day were light and simple in the old-fashioned way), in summer when he was not too busy he would often lie in the sun, and a book was read aloud while he made notes and extracts. He made extracts of everything he read, and always said that there was no book so bad that some good could not be got out of it. After his rest in the sun he generally took a cold bath, and then ate something and had a short sleep; after which he worked till dinner time as if he had started on a new day. A book was read aloud during the meal and he took rapid notes. I remember that one of his friends told a reader to go back and repeat a word he had mispronounced. "Couldn't you understand him?" said my uncle. His friend admitted that he could. "Then why make him go back? Your interruption has lost us at least ten lines." To such lengths did he carry his passion for saving time. In summer he rose from dinner while it was still light, in winter as soon as darkness fell, as if some law compelled him.

This was his routine in the midst of his public duties and the bustle of the city. In the country, the only time he took from his work was for his bath, and by bath I mean his actual immersion, for while he was being rubbed down and dried he had a book read to him or dictated notes. When travelling he felt free from other responsibilities to give every minute to his work; he kept a secretary at his side with book and notebook, and in winter saw that his hands were protected by long sleeves, so that even bitter weather could not rob him of a working hour. For the same reason, too, he used to be carried about Rome in a chair. I can remember how he scolded me for walking; according to him I need not have wasted those hours, for he thought any time wasted which was not devoted to work. It was this application which enabled him to finish all those volumes, and to leave me 160 notebooks of selected passages, written in a minute hand on both sides of the page, so that their number really doubled. He used to say that when he was serving as a procurator in Spain he could have sold those notebooks to Larcius Licinus for 400,000 sesterces, and there were far fewer of them then.

When you consider the extent of his reading and writing I wonder if you feel that he could have never been a public official or a friend of the Emperor, but on the other hand, now that you know of his application, that he should have achieved more? In fact his official duties put every possible obstacle in his path; and yet there was nothing which his energy could not surmount. So I cannot help smiling when anyone calls me studious, for compared with him I am the idlest of men. And yet perhaps I am not, seeing that so much of my time is taken with official work and service to my friends. Any one of your lifelong devotees of literature, if put alongside my uncle, would blush to feel themselves thus enslaved to sleep and idleness.

I have let my letter run on, though I intended only to answer your question about the books left by my uncle. However, I feel sure that reading these details will give you as much pleasure as the actual books, and may even spur you on to the ambition of doing more than read them, if you can produce something similar yourself.

To Cornelius Tacitus (Book Six, 16)

Thank you for asking me to send you a description of my uncle's death so that you can leave an accurate account of it for posterity; I know that immortal fame awaits him if his death is recorded by you. Is it true that he perished in a catastrophe which destroyed the loveliest regions of the earth, a fate shared by whole cities and their people, and one so memorable that it is likely to make his name live forever: and he himself wrote a number of books of lasting value: but you write for all time and can still do much to perpetuate his memory. The fortunate man, in my opinion, is he to whom the gods have granted the power to do something which is worth recording or to write what is worth reading, and most fortunate of all is the man who can do both. Such a man was my uncle, as his own books and yours will prove. So you set me a task I would choose for myself, and I am more than willing to start on it.

My uncle was stationed in Misenum, in active command of the fleet. On 24 August, in the early afternoon, my mother drew his attention to a cloud of unusual size and appearance. He had been out in the sun, had taken a cold bath, and lunched while lying down, and was then working at his books. He called for his shoes and climbed up to a place which would give him the best view of the phenomenon. It was not clear at that distance from which mountain the cloud was rising (it was afterwards known to be Vesuvius); its general appearance can best be expressed as being like an umbrella pine, for it rose to a great height on a sort of trunk and then split off into branches, I imagine because it was thrust upwards by the first blast and then left unsupported as the pressure subsided, or else was borne down by its own weight so that it spread out and gradually dispersed. Sometimes it looked white, sometimes blotched and dirty, according to the amount of soil and ashes it carried with it. My uncle's scholarly acumen saw at once that it was important enough for a closer inspection, and he ordered a boat to be made ready, telling me I could come with him if I wished. I replied that I preferred to go on with my studies, and as it happened he had himself given me some writing to do.

As he was leaving the house he was handed a message from Rectina, wife of Tascius whose house was at the foot of the mountain, so that escape was impossible except by boat. She was terrified of the danger threatening her and implored him to rescue her from her fate. He changed his plans, and what he had begun in a spirit of inquiry he completed as a hero. He gave orders for the warships to be launched and went on board himself with the intention of bringing help to many more people besides Rectina, for this lovely stretch of coast was thickly populated. He hurried to the place which everyone else was hastily leaving, steering his course straight for the danger zone. He was entirely fearless, describing each new movement and phase of the portent to be noted down exactly as he observed them. Ashes were already falling, hotter and thicker as the ships drew near, followed by bits of pumice and blackened stone, charred and cracked by the flames: then suddenly they were in shallow water, and the shore was blocked by the debris from the mountain. For a moment my uncle wondered whether to turn back, but when the helmsman advised this he refused, telling him that Fortune stood by the courageous and they must make for Pomponianus at Stabiae. He was cut off there by the breadth of the bay (for the shore gradually curves round a basin filled by the sea) so that he was not as yet in danger, though it was clear that this would come nearer as it spread. Pomponianus had therefore already put his belongings on board ship, intending to escape if the contrary wind fell. This wind was of course full in my uncle's favour, and he was able to bring his ship in. He embraced his terrified friend, cheered and encouraged him, and thinking he could calm his fears by showing his own composure, gave orders that he was to be carried to the bathroom. After his bath he lay down and dined; he was quite cheerful, or at any rate pretended he was, which was no less courageous.

Meanwhile on Mount Vesuvius broad sheets of fire and leaping flames blazed at several points, their bright glare emphasized by the darkness of night. My uncle tried to allay the fears of his companions by repeatedly declaring that these were nothing but bonfires left by the peasants in their terror, or else empty houses on fire in the districts they had abandoned. Then he went on to rest and certainly slept, for as he was a stout man his breathing was rather loud and heavy and could be heard by people coming and going outside his door. By this time the courtyard giving access to his room was full of ashes mixed with pumice-stones, so that its level had risen, and if he had stayed in the room any longer he would never have got out. He was wakened, came out and joined Pomponianus and the rest of the household who had sat up all night. They debated whether to stay indoors or take their chance in the open, for the buildings were now shaking with violent shocks, and seemed to be swaying to and fro as if they were torn from their foundations. Outside on the other hand, there was the danger of falling pumice-stones, even though these were light and porous; however, after comparing the risks they chose the latter. In my uncle's case one reason outweighed the other, but for the others it was a choice of fears. As protection against falling objects they put pillows on their heads tied down with cloths.

Elsewhere there was daylight by this time, but they were still in darkness, blacker and denser than any ordinary night, which they relieved by lighting torches and various kinds of lamp. My uncle decided to go down to the shore and investigate on the spot the possibility of any escape by sea, but he found the waves still wild and dangerous. A sheet was spread on the ground for him to lie down, and he repeatedly asked for cold water to drink. Then the flames and smell of sulphur which gave warning of approaching fire drove the others to take flight and roused him to stand up. He stood leaning on two slaves and then suddenly collapsed, I imagine because the dense fumes choked his breathing by blocking his windpipe which was constitutionally weak and narrow and often inflamed. When daylight returned on the 26th—two days after the last day he had seen—his body was found intact and uninjured, still fully clothed and looking more like sleep than death.

Meanwhile my mother and I were at Misenum, but this is not of any historic interest, and you only wanted to hear about my uncle's death. I will say no more, except to add that I have described in detail every incident which I either witnessed myself or heard about immediately after the event, when reports were most likely to be accurate. It is for you to select what best suits your purpose, for there is a great difference between a letter to a friend and history written for all to read.